Boyfriends

KEYONIA DAWSON

Contents

CHAPTER 1:

The Beginning

It all started so innocently and pure. Love at first sight, type shit. That puppy love that never really fades away. He was always there and always supportive. This is part of the reason his spot can't be replaced, but the honesty is what sets him apart and guarantees him a place in my heart, if not my entire heart. The first day I met him, I got jitters and couldn't help but blush on the inside. It was a feeling I never felt before. Butterflies started rushing through my stomach, and I instantly became shy. Things that would normally flow out like my name/number were now my stumbling blocks in the way of my future. We met at the skating rink on a Friday night. It's crazy because the rink was packed, and he was trying to get another girl's attention at the time we met. He asked me if I knew where she was. "Chuckles to myself"," when I looked up at this handsome piece of caramel in front of me, it's like we both felt something or could see something so great within one another. He instantly changed his mind about finding the girl, and we exchanged numbers. Being that we were young and lived in the two different cities, my time with him was limited and cut short after every skating rink visit on Fridays. This caused us to only be friends, but because of the feelings felt, we soon united and became inseparable. Everything changed my freshman year of high school. My father got a new job at the high school where Jason went to school.

Although I lived in a different city, my dad could register me because he was employed in the school district. I had two options: I could attend high school down the street from my house or down the street from my future hubby's house. I decided to start fresh and attend HHS in August with my dad. I didn't tell Jason I would be attending the same school as him. I wanted it to be a surprise. Simply because we were crushing. I wasn't even sure if he liked me as much as I liked him. Or whether he has other girls at his school who felt the same way I felt or more for him. I didn't want to appear clingy. My mind over analyzes a situation all the time, so I decided to just show up at school and act like he acts. If he sees me and doesn't speak, I know to keep it moving. Only time would tell. The whole summer, I enjoyed life and anticipated seeing his reaction in the cafeteria, or hallway, or office. I couldn't help but imagine. School started on August 6th . It was a beautiful sunny day. My dad woke up yelling, "stop moving like you have a car and career already. You are broke, baby, and I am leaving in 40 minutes." I literally rolled out of bed and hit the floor. My hair was already freshly flat -ironed. All I had to do was take a quick shower, brush my teeth, get dressed, and grab my bag. I did all of that in twenty minutes and fixed an omelet in 6 minutes. It was so good, and I was halfway finished with it before I locked the door to get in the car with my rude ass father.

The drive to HHS was twenty-five minutes away, so I had no choice but to hurry. I didn't want to be the "late new kid" who walked in while the teacher was in the middle of calling the role. I went to sleep shortly after I fastened my seatbelt. It felt like I blinked for two seconds, and the car was pulling into the parking lot of the school. I quickly wiped the drool from my face and adjusted my uniform. I jumped out and locked the door because my dad was obviously in a rush. He didn't even wake me up.

I run to the office as the alarm goes off on the car. My dad's car is all new and stupid. If someone locks you in the car, and you get out and relock the door, the alarm goes off. I guess it thinks someone is stealing it. I dashed through a crowd of students because everyone was now staring at me and my dad's screaming car. I texted him and told him about the car, and this fool says, "handled it. Bring me your phone . There is no phone policy here." I left him on read, retrieved my schedule, and started looking for my first block class.

My schedule read:
1st History 101- Maple
2nd Algebra 101-Dixen
3rd Art 101-Sampson
4th Biology 101Roberts.

I asked the guidance counselor were the room numbers available, and she replied, "Teachers' names are located on their doors." To my surprise, they all were. That was so convenient. The first and second blocks ran smoothly. I didn't even get sleepy. Even though what all the teachers discussed were the rubric and handbook., I hadn't seen Jason, but I also haven't had time to look. All I could think about was lunch. I walked two halls over from the math hall to get to the art hall, and it felt like a mile. I thought I was going to die before lunchtime. I walked in and sat straight down at the first seat I saw. Because instead of desks, he had two large tables. They could seat 15 people per table. I never looked up at anyone in the class. The teacher was doing his own thing, and so was I. I decided to sleep during class and wake up during lunchtime.

Lunch started at 12:45 for us. I was walking by 12:40, not giving a care what was going on around me. I grabbed my lunch money, lunch box and purse, then head to the cafeteria rather sluggish. I got in line like the rest of the students, but I noticed some dude is rather close behind me. I didn't turn and stare because I don't feel like making conversation. As the line in front of us grows shorter, we finally entered the doorway to be served. The young man behind me says, "So, lunch box plus extra lunch? I never knew you were so greedy, Anna." I turned slowly, and there was Jason. I almost pissed my pants. "Well, Jason, you don't really know me"," I replied. "Guess I'm about to get to know you, being that we will see each other more" says Jason. "I saw you in class, but you were knocked out slobbering." From that day on, we ate lunch together, skipped class together, lied together, partied together, and even cheated together. *laughs loudly* All the innocence went out the window when we finally kissed. We were sitting in the classroom talking about our project, and suddenly, he grabbed my face so sweetly and kissed me. Everything felt so real, so private, so new…, and I didn't know how to feel. I just knew feelings were hitting me left to right. I would love to say it stopped there, but it didn't. With his eyes on me, he whispered, "Watch Mr. Frank and act as if you're doing your work." We didn't have desks. We had tables. He slowly unzipped my uniform pants.

While leaving them buttoned, he slipped his fingers inside of my pants and started to do things with his fingers that made it harder than ever for me to keep a straight face and hold my composure. I just kept thinking how the fuck. Why the fuck? When the fuck? I just didn't understand why it felt so good, and why haven't I experienced this before. How can something so wrong feel so right? By the time I snapped back from my thoughts, I was ready to marry him, kiss him, run away with him, ALL OF THE ABOVE. When I looked at Jason, he smiled as if he knew he had touched my soul. I know that he knows he grabbed my soul instead of my vagina.

Time continued to wind down throughout the school year. Before I knew it, we are in the middle of my sophomore year, and I find myself in the girl's restroom with the lights off standing face to face with Jason. My heart is racing because first, I know what he did under the table in class. Just imagine what he'll do while we're alone in a half -empty school, in a vacant restroom. I wasn't mad, and I damn sure wasn't going to stop him. But my biggest fear was to be caught by an administrator and must be asked to call my father. That's a risk I kind of had to take, though. Now or never type of shit. This time he unfastened my pants and slid them down quietly. Then he picked me up and sat me on the sink. He kissed me, then whispered, "you ok?' I replied, "yes." He then kissed me and whispered, "It's going to hurt a little, I'm going to go slow." As promised, he did go slow, and it did hurt a little bit. The pain never really bothered me because I was prepared, and he took his time. So, the experience was great and new, but again, back to my thoughts, Where are the teachers, principals, hell anybody. I'm not in distress, but I'll just get up. So, I instantly stopped him after four minutes and got dressed. A janitor walked past the door as we were coming out. Me being me, I thought aww shit, I'm about to be drenched in holy oil, whoopings, punishments, and long skirts. This fool looked at both of us, smiled, then said, "Hey, have a nice day." I was only gonna lie and say, I left my pads in the classroom, and he had to bring them to me due to no other girls being present. As the years went by, the only things that changed between us were age, locations, and the desire to be with one another. 24/7. I moved twenty minutes away, and he moved to a new home in the same city he had been living in.

CHAPTER 2:

Promise Rings & Broken things

Ever felt pain when everything was numb? I can give so many ways and reasons as to how and why this could take place. I'll only name a few. Just enough to get your heart racing, brain pumping, and blood boiling. The number one and most common way to experience and encounter such discomfort is to catch your loved one cheating. Going through your man's phone and finding every truth that he presented to you as a lie is the second way. You end up finding shit you didn't even have a clue he was capable of. You begin counting that nigga hour at work and adding them to the number of hours he spends with you just to try and find the time he created to be with another bitch. Men manage their time -wise as fuck. They don't care if they have to give each person an hour worth of dick. Boy, can they ruffle a girl's feathers! It's like the lies hit you in the pit of your stomach, and you start to replay and rethink every single thing the man you used to trust has said, whether past or present. When a man lies, I don't give a fuck if he says, "it's raining'," I'm going to double -check. It doesn't just cease overnight. The pain slowly goes from your stomach to your chest, and if you overthink things like I do, it will eventually take over your head. You will get an emotional headache. I'm not saying this to start a -she -girl men haters club against all men. Just to explain some of the feelings and emotions that I experienced throughout my emotional love coaster. The headaches and heartbreaks are what separates the women from the girls. It seemed as if the older we grew, the harder it became to balance and maintain a healthy relationship that was mutually beneficial.

Although we were growing older chronologically, we were still young mentally. A person's chronological age could be twenty while mentally their age could be that of a sixteen -year -old. I notice this in a lot of guys. Women don't really want to appear younger until they hit their mid to late thirties. We were around the age of eighteen or nineteen when things really start to test our faith in one another. That's when our relationship began to get rocky. There were times when he would simply kiss my forehead, and an ocean would appear in my panties. A fire within my soul, chemistry so strong that we would begin to miss one another before we departed. Everything changed for the worse when we went off to two separate colleges. I decided to complete two years at a community college close to home . Meanwhile, he decided a four -year university eight hours away was best for him. We spent as much time as we could together in the summer before freshman year was about to start. We also promised to visit one another and continue our relationship as is. We started school in August, and he came home to visit in October. I told him that the next trip I would take was to visit him. Due to my balancing work and school, I wasn't able to visit until December. I planned this romantic surprise weekend trip. I bought rose petals, candles, chocolate -covered strawberries, lingerie, handcuffs, and whipped crème. Just know I was prepared to give my man the ultimate weekend of his life. So I wake up early Friday around 8:00 am and started getting dressed. Once dressed, I loaded my car and got on the road. Halfway through the drive, I called my boyfriend, and he doesn't answer. I think nothing of it because he does have class and work to attend. The closer I get to arriving, the more my stomach aches. I picked up my cell and called again because, at this point, you should have texted me to see how my day was, or just if I'm alive. Like I honestly could be bent over throwing nothing but ass, and you're missing.

After eight long hours, I arrive. Thank God, his grandma sent me the address. My surprise would be an epic fail without her. As I roll my luggage and goody bags up to the door, I notice someone who looks familiar from Jason's photos. I approach the 6'2 clean -cut, muscular male whose abs are nothing short of amazing. As I introduce myself,

I can't help but to notice his beautiful, cunning smile. He looked like a handsome, slick fox. It was as if his smile hid deeper intentions, but what do I know, I just met the guy. I asked him if he knew Jason Jackson. He smiled cunningly again and said, "Yes, we're roommates. I will show you how to get to our room." As we walk to the room, he makes general conversation, but I noticed he never once mentioned his name. I'm cautiously answering the questions that he asks me, such as," "so, what are you doing tonight?" I don't understand why that matters if he can't even tell me his name. The closer we get to the end of the hall, the louder these noises are getting. Right when the noise becomes embarrassingly loud as fuck, I realized someone is fucking really loud. I turn to look at no name, and he unlocks the door where the noises seem to be coming from.

With tear -filled eyes, a racing and shattered heart, and a mind full of killer thoughts, I watch as my man drops pure dick into the soul of another bitch. They were so wrapped up at the moment that they didn't even hear us enter. I was such an emotional wreck as I pulled my taser out of my purse and put it on the highest voltage power. I hit his ass from the back with that bitch. He almost ran the anonymous hoe straight through the wall. She started off with her back arched and him pounding her from the back, but when I got done with their dumb asses, you would have thought they were in the circus. They hit a couple of flips that landed him on his back and her under the damn tv stand. I whooped that bitch for twenty minutes then zapped their ass again. I eventually left but couldn't help but think about finding no name roommate, so I could zap his ass too. Call me "THE ZAPSTER, HOE.." Because for one, he set me up and took off when I spazzed out. Now, what if I was the type of female that got totally out of control and took shit too far? That's why he was doing all that sly ass smiling.

Jason was texting my phone, swearing to God that his roommate only did that cause he really liked the hoe Jason was fucking. I just want to know WHAT THE FUCK that got to do with my reasons for being mad ? Not a bitch ass thing. I don't really care because everybody was getting their asses zapped for trying to play me on some weak shit.

When I got outside, this fool was sitting in the same damn spot I met him in. Good looking out Satan, cause I know God ain't set no malicious shit like this up. It was the devil. I slowly crept behind him and placed the Taser against his back so he would know it was me. I placed my lips as close as I could to his ear and whispered "BITCH, I could really make you dance for that shit you pulled, but I needed to know, so I guess I'll just make you feel my wrath." He better be glad I used the majority of my power on Jason and his mistress. He didn't feel half of what they felt. But of course, God doesn't like ugly, so my ugly ass must have done something that he didn't like. I ended up manless, carless, and heartbroken. Carless because while I was inside for thirty minutes, whooping ass, my car was being towed!

CHAPTER 3:

Blessings & Lessons

I sat on a bench nearby and texted Summer, Kaylee, and Brielle to catch them up on the latest bull shit in my life. When I opened the group message, I noticed that they had already texted me. Kaylee: You made it BFF?

Summer: I just woke up, I got my backbeat in last night, but anyway, you made it Tootie? Cause if not, your BFF will be OTW!

Brielle: Best friend, just let me know you made it safely dang! You love acting funny when you're cuddled up.

Me: Sorry for not calling when I made it. I've been here for an hour, and so far, I've caught my man fucking another woman. I tazed and kicked their asses. Tazed Jason's roommate, and had my car towed in a city that's unfamiliar to me. I think I've accomplished enough bull shit in that hour to last me a lifetime. My dad is going to kill me.

Brielle: I just transferred three hundred dollars to your account, and if Kaylee and Summer send nothing, those bitches ARE NOT YOUR FRIENDS.

Summer: Bitch, first of all, Kaylee, and I have cash on us, so we're both OTW to wire Anna Bella seven hundred dollars altogether.

Kaylee: It took me a minute to respond because I'm trying to make sure I'll have enough money in my bank account in order to get up there to fucking fight.

Me: OMG! Have y'all been stripping while I was gone? Thanks, so much, by the way, I'm about to catch a cab to get the money and go to the tow truck company. I love y'all! They all replied, "I love you more."

My phone died right after I read their text messages. As I sat on the bench, I prayed the day doesn't get any worse, and up walks a chocolate piece of goodness with eyes so captivating that I almost forgot I have problems and should stay focused. His teeth were so white they were damn near the same color as his lab coat that I almost overlooked because of his beautiful eyes. I was staring, and I didn't give a fuck because no one that sexy should go unattended. Skin so creamy you melt from just looking. Not to mention, he's damn near 6"3 and not all bones. I can tell from his freshly lined up beard, extra sparkly Rolex, and white coat that he was a clean-cut paid snack. The only thing I couldn't figure out was why his paid ass was spending time near this bench. Is he waiting on a ride or a cab? Even if he was, that doesn't make him broke, but if I was carless, that Rolex would be my down payment. Distracted by my thoughts, I failed to control my facial expressions. The rather handsome man burst into laughter and made eye contact. He asked, "What's a beautiful young woman like you doing with a mind full of stressful thoughts?" "Just trying to figure out how I'm going to get to the tow shop to get my car." I replied. In my head,I know my mind was far from that car, and all on this man in front of me, but I wasn't going to tell him that. " Are you waiting for a cab ?" I ask. He replies, "No, I came over here to get your name, and number, but you appeared to be in deep thought." He offered me a ride and told me he would love to get to know me. Hesitant at first, I said no, then I remembered my tazer was fully charged. As we walk through the parking lot, I'm praying his car has no complications nor problems, and this man hit the unlock button, and the lights on a Bugatti Chiron came on. It was all black with black tinted windows and black rims.

The seats were white while the dashboard and other interior items were marble with mixtures of greys, whites, and blacks. The car is such a beauty, but I hope he doesn't think it's going to get him the booty. As we ride, he makes general conversation, but I can't remember anything past his age and name because I'm making a photographic memory of the street names and stores that we passed just in case he gets crazy. He said his name was Jaxon West, but his friends call him Kash. A part of me wants to know why they call him that, and the other part just wants to assume he is a well-paid doctor. I'll worry about that after I get my car. We rode for twenty minutes before pulling into Billy's tow shop, where cars are towed on the spot. No wonder my baby got towed so fast. They probably spotted me before I even thought about parking. As I looked up to thank Jaxon, I noticed he was smiling again, but this time, he's handing me six-hundred dollars. Puzzled as fuck, I said, "Thank you, but no thank you. I owe you for giving me a ride. You've been more than generous, and I'm thankful." He smirked in a flirtatious way, then reached over as if he was going to kiss me and slid the six hundred in my purse. Jaxon then got out the car, paid the tow man, handed me my keys and all. He then added, "You are way too beautiful to be stressing. Drop that lost nigga and get a boss nigga.

Matter of fact, get yourself a grown man. You ain't even mine, but I want to give you the world. I hate that stressed look on you, so call me whenever about whatever, it doesn't matter." Jaxon said that, and I got super wet. I didn't know what to do or say, so I said thank you and gave him a hug. He embraced me, then ran his fingers through my hair, and kissed my forehead. I never felt so secure in my life. I let go but didn't really want to. So, I suggested that we go out to eat before I got back on the road. Puzzled by something I said, Jaxon asked, "Where are you going?" He replied, "Home, I live eight hours away." Just when I think life couldn't get any better, Jaxon asked me to stay. He said that his house had plenty of space and that I could have his room, and he'd pick another if I wanted him to. I did want my own room if I was to stay. I quickly agreed and followed him home after I began to charge my phone. We pulled into the driveway, and the house is nothing short of amazing. Jaxon's house was like a castle with big welcoming windows, and the flowers complemented the house so well. Yard and house of the year type shit. The garden of rose bushes was so big and vibrant that they automatically caught my eye. The roses were bloodshot red, well-trimmed, and kept up. The lawn was freshly cut, and nothing could top the wrap -around balcony on the second floor of the house. The balcony was all glass like the ones that usually overlooked the beach and wrapped all the way around the house. I was so overwhelmed that I just decided to contain my excitement. "Your home is lovely!", I stated while Jaxon assisted me with carrying my bags inside. He said, "Thank you, but I still say the best view is the one I have right now. I know that my time with you may be limited, so pick a room, whichever one you want and freshen up and make yourself at home. We could get dressed and go out, eat take out and watch movies, or I'll cook your dinner, and we could watch movies and get to know one another. It's whatever you want, just give me a chance to cater to you in ways that'll help your nights and days run smoother."

CHAPTER 4:

Priceless Distractions

As I stand in this luxurious shower that's hitting me from three different directions, I run my hands through my long curly coils and almost drift into a slumber. The water was steamy and felt as if it washed away all the dirt, baggage, and stress all together. I honestly don't want to get out, but the least I could do is have dinner with the man who has basically seen a crown over my head and wings on my back since he met me. After an hour, I decided to get out and put my pajamas on. I hope I'm not underdressed for dinner. I left my room to look for Jaxon, but when I got close to his room, I heard the shower. So, I decided to explore the second floor while he showers. Of course, I picked a room downstairs. This allows me to be close to the exit and the kitchen. The stairs meet at the bottom , but as they go up, they form two staircases that provide an exit on both the right and left side of the second floor. Coming down the stairs must feel like you're entering a ballroom and you're Cinderella. As I get closer to the top of the staircase, I noticed something blue and lit up. It was a built-in wall aquarium that stretched more than halfway down the hall. It was full of all types of tropical fish, reefs, seashells, and starfish. The aquarium was so captivating. There were so many colors and so much beauty in one tank. The water was so clear that I could see every detail on every fish. The plants that lay at the bottom even looked full of life as if they were waving. Interrupted by the sound of my host's footsteps as he comes to join me in awe, I scold myself in my head.

Too busy looking at the fish that I forgot to listen out for the shower to stop. I asked, "what's for dinner?" Without taking my eyes off the aquarium. "Depends on what you have a taste for'," Jaxon replied. I turned around and said, "since it's up to me, I want breakfast." I almost said in bed when I turned around, and he was shirtless in his Gucci swim trunks. He is beautifully and wonderfully made. God took his time when making and molding this man. They should have nicknamed him Gold because that's what I saw when looking at him. Skin so golden and perfect that it made me wonder where that fountain of youth was that he possibly drank from? His abs look like he eats the gym for breakfast. I guess he can read minds too because he looked at me and said, "I don't fuck on the first night, but I'll have my chef cook you breakfast. Come take a dive in the pool with me until then, or just keep me company." He grabbed my hand so gently and led the way. I wanted to do nothing more than submit and marry this walking piece of heaven. The indoor pool, which I didn't expect to be indoors nor on the first floor, reminded me of a mini Niagara Falls. It was like a mini getaway on a mini island of a huge castle. He had palm trees and real coconuts for drinking. The indoor pool has two bars. One outside of the pool, and the other inside the pool. "Where the fuck do you work??" I asked as I rethink my decision to not swim. This would be a perfect opportunity to play with his head and find out if he was going to stay true to his word. "I am the only cardiovascular surgeon in this city and surrounding areas. I mainly work from the hospital behind the bench you were sitting on, but I often must travel due to the fact that I am the only surgeon in the city." Jaxon explained right before diving in the middle of the pool. He swam like a dolphin. The water rolled off his back as if he and the water were one. I just wonder if he's sent from God or Satan. Only time will tell.

He swam for an hour and a half before getting out. I now understand why he looks like he eats a gym for breakfast, lunch, and dinner. Afterward, he changed clothes, and we had a candlelit brunch in the movie room. I'm starting to believe he doesn't have sex on the first night because, after the first night, his dates rape him. I don't know many doctors with movie theatres in their homes, but then again, I only know the doctors who treat me. I don't even know them that well now that I think of it. We watched "John Wick" and ate chicken, waffles, and scrambled eggs. Which was splendid and just what I needed to relax a little. An action movie and a meal. Towards the middle of the movie, my feet and back start to ache, so I start massaging my right foot to relieve the tension. Jaxon looked at me as if I was in error or had stolen the movie screen. Confused by his facial expressions, I ask, "what, what is it?" He stood, turned the movie off, then grabbed my hand, and said, "follow me so I can show you." He led me to his room, picked me up, and put me on the bed, then began to massage my feet. "The problem is, you don't know how you're supposed to be treated." "When you're with me, you don't have to lift a finger for nothing, not even to feed yourself if you don't want to!" he said. I was at a loss for words, so I just shook my head yes. He started massaging my feet, then my thighs, and eventually ended on my back. His bed and the massage felt so good that I drifted off into a slumber so deep that if he did get some of my goodies, I didn't even care.

CHAPTER 5

Reflections

I wake up the next morning with endless texts and calls from Jason. Too bad, his ass is going on the block list. I feel too good to deal with old trash. Let the garbage man handle that. Oh my gosh, he's calling again. *Answers the phone* "Jason, it's a beautiful day to hoe, so enjoy the block list hoe." *hangs up and adds Jason to the block list* That felt good, simply because I'm over it. You always know when you're done, because you no longer use your energy to fight, argue, and discuss things that you know you can't change. You begin to evolve in a way that you can almost feel. It's like removing the dark cloud of wonder and curiosity out of your life and just living to the fullest. I wonder what my future holds, but then again, I'll just find out when the time comes. My biggest problem at this moment is when you begin to show a guy you care about him. That's when he starts to show you that he doesn't. I rolled over to see if Jaxon was in bed. I never checked before answering the phone for Jason. How fucking rude? Thank God he wasn't in bed. I got up to use the restroom and to brush my teeth and in comes Jaxon with a dozen pink roses, breakfast surrounded by strawberries and cream on a gold platter, and a beautiful day dress. Tears start pouring down my face. I thought to myself, how could a total stranger put their life on hold to cater to mine?

"What's wrong, dry your eyes and get dressed. I wanna take you shopping." Jaxon said. He dried my eyes and bear hugged me gently. I never felt so secure in a strangers arms. I decided to postpone my goodbye until after our little date. I got dressed and met him at the car where he was waiting on the passenger side in order to open my door.

After making sure I was safe and sound, he drove us to this beautiful beach and started leading me towards the water. "I'm not going swimming!" I explained as he looks to be enjoying my suspense. "I know you're not; we're going sailing." He said. It's like I instantly got seasick, and I wasn't even on the sea yet. I know he could tell by my facial expressions and lack of movement towards the water. He laughed uncontrollably like I was the funniest joke ever. When done, he asked, "Why that face? It'll be romantic, fun, and private." I explained how I have never been on a boat due to my dad's fear of me drowning. "Jaxon, I don't think I can. When I was five years old, my mom drowned trying to save me. We have a lake behind our house that my dad would always fish in. The water was always so pretty, and I always wanted to touch it. I guess that's what led me to dive in."

"My father had two choices. One was to save me, and the other was to save my mother. Either way, he knew he couldn't do both, but he was willing to try." Jaxon apologized for bringing old memories to life, then asked what I would like to do. I decided to conquer my fears after ten minutes of pacing back and forth from the yacht without getting aboard. At first, I felt sick, but a part of me knew that Jaxon wouldn't let anything harm me. Twenty minutes into the boat ride, I began to relax and exchange conversation as Jaxon pours us both a glass of wine. "Come here!" he says, as if we're not sitting across from each other. I respond, "come where?" Come and sit on my lap and leave all your worries behind. The problem is that you think too much, which causes you to worry too much instead of enjoying the moments worth living for.." I had no choice but to get up and go sit in his lap. Everything he said made sense. I spend too much time thinking about the past and things I can't change.

From this moment on, I'm going to live for me. Before I could sit down, he started taking everything out of his pockets. Usually, when men do this, they pull out a wallet, phone, condoms, and maybe a pocketknife. Not Jaxon, he pulled so much money from each of his pockets. I started to think I saw things due to the wine. He had four pockets, and it seems like they held four-thousand dollars each. When done, he handed the money to me and said, "Put this in your purse sweetheart and come get comfortable." I'm not going to ask any questions at this point. I'm just going to put the money up and relax. As I sat in his lap and watched the sunset, I became super turned on by the way he's holding me and kissing my head. I slowly get up and tell Jaxon I'm going to the restroom. I took a quick shower then placed my roses Jaxon got me all over the room. Kind of nervous because I've only had sex with Jason, and Jaxon is someone I just met. I think to myself, "Fuck that!"and began to walk back to the promenade deck where Jaxon was.

I know he'll be surprised when I walk up to him naked. We're the only people on this extravagant cruise, so we might as well make it exciting. So what if the captain sees me. He'll never see me again after today. As I get closer to Jaxon, I heard him having a very business-like conversation, but it doesn't sound like hospital talk. Something like "A brick is a brick, and even if they don't have it, then you know to use the stick." Confused and horny, I continued with my agenda. As soon as I got in front of him, he stopped talking on the phone and instantly threw it into the water. The sweetest thing a guy could do is to put you ahead of anyone else in his life. Drowning his phone made me know that when it comes to me, I get his undivided attention. Without saying a word, he picked me up and began to kiss me, and he carried me to the room. The love felt real and unreal at the same time. As I lay on the bed, Jaxon kissed every inch of my body and made sure to end with my vagina. So overwhelmed and overly stressed, I reached my climax in five minutes, and instantly felt like my soul left my body and jumped into Jaxon's pockets. I didn't mind; I just never had that much stress lifted off me in such a short time. When finished with the rest of his meal, he slid his penis in slowly and the rest was magic.

CHAPTER 6:

Dreams & Realities

I woke up feeling rejuvenated as I enjoyed a full body massage in bed. Jaxon really sets the bar high, and I didn't know how to leave him. I'm not leaving because he's wronged me. I'm leaving because I can't just pick up and leave my life behind. I live hours away from him, and I honestly don't know where my trust would stand once I make it home and face reality. My thoughts were interrupted when I received a message from my group chat.

Summer: When are you coming home? I miss you.

Brielle: ??

Kaylee: Right??

Me: I'm going to leave tomorrow early in the morning,. I met a very nice guy, who I needed some alone time with. I'll fill y'all in when I get home.

Kaylee: OMG! I've been waiting to tell y'all, but I met a nice man too, who happens to be a dealer. He's so tall, handsome, and chocolate.

Summer: Meanwhile, I've been a hoe. I got a socket and a plug. My socket gone treat me like a queen and buy me anything, then turn around and tell me to hold the pack down while he goes out of town. I love it that way. My plug can come over and spend the night, and we'll get high as a kite off the sockets pack lmao.

Brielle: When do I get to meet these lucky men before or after Summer's funeral?

Me: LOL! I cannot deal!. I look forward to meeting them as well, and I'm happy for you, Kaylee.

Kaylee: My guy lives 8 or 9 hours away, so I'm not sure . I hope we'll all plan one big get together. Summer, make sure you pick one guy to bring the socket or the plug lol.

Summer: LOL! It's all fun and games until I sell the pack and use the money to move away. I'm about to go pop up on one of my dudes then take a nap. Anna, send a text or call when you leave.

Me: I'll send everyone a text. I love y'all. TTYL!

Brielle: I love you too.

Kaylee: I love you more.

Jaxon ends the massage with soul snatching back kisses. If only he could see the love in my eyes now. I've never been catered for in the ways Jaxon caters to me. "You know you really make me feel like a million dollars, but "I gotta go, Jaxon." I explained. Jaxon replied, "I feel like you're worth way more than that. That's why I treat you like my most prized possession. Only a grown man knows when he has something worth fighting for." "I hate when you say things like that. The things you say and words you use always make me want to just live my life from your arms for the rest of my life Jax I replied. "It's so cute how you call me Jax, my Grandma calls me that, but please stay sweetheart. Money is never an issue, and I'll buy you a place to stay if you don't want to live with me. I'll even pay to send all your things from home" says Jaxon. "I refuse to put all of my worries and baggage on you. How about we keep communicating and building our friendship. We could take turns visiting one another and video chatting. Let's start there and see where we go." I insist. Hesitant at first, Jaxon finally agrees. "I'll agree to allow you to leave under a few conditions. " Jaxon said as he held me tightly. "What is it, babe. I owe you the world for how great you've treated me." Jaxon smiled then kissed me on the forehead before making his requests known. "For starters, I want to hear from you every day." Jaxon insisted that the last day be extra special and wanted us to spend the last day without our phones. Lastly, he said that he wanted me to do nothing but relax and let him spoil me. He told me that there could be no overthinking today and that I couldn't even worry about what tomorrow had in store. Jaxon wanted me to be totally relaxed.

"I'll make sure you get home safely." he insisted. "No problem." I replied. He grabbed my hand and kissed it and told me, "I got you forever," if you call, I'm coming." All I could do was hug and kiss him because I knew it was true. We get up and get dressed to get off the yacht, and as soon as we get to the exit, Jaxon asks to blindfold me. I laughed, then agree with the gesture. Even though I'm wearing a blindfold, I feel completely comfortable with holding Jaxon's hand as he leads me to cupid knows where. I just pray I don't come back to him nine months later, holding his child due to the romantically explicit weekend. He may be paid, but bitches get played like spades every day.

Jax led me to the car and picked me up and put me in. He told the driver to take us to the places they had already discussed. I sat in the back seat of this car, praying they aren't on any human trafficking type shit, because I would hate to taze this man due to how kind he has been, but I will. We spent at least thirty minutes traveling to our destination. I could not say for sure because Jax kind of made me promise to spend our last day phoneless. Besides, I would not have been able to view the time anyway, wearing a blindfold. The time we did spend in the car got me thinking about how I haven't heard from my dad since I left home. Honestly, I was worried, but a soon as I heard this male voice say, "Welcome to Cartier!" I forgot about everything. My mind started to go crazy. I know the cheapest bracelet they could possibly have is four-thousand, and it only gets higher. I don't have two-thousand dollars, let alone four. Why are we in here? I can't ask Jaxon because I'm at a loss for words. My mouth is not working. I reach for my blindfold, and Jaxon instantly grabbed my hand gently and said, "Stop bae, hold your wrist out so these nice people can bless my little baby." Keep your blindfold on until we reach our destination." he insisted. After trying a few on, Jaxon finally said, "that one will do, what's the price." The associates replies, "One moment, sir." He began to type on the register to price and calculate the total cost of the item. The jewelry consultant finally said, "forty-two thousand dollars and seventy-two cents." I almost dropped to my knees and proposed to him. Because still at a loss for words, I stood there in awe. It wasn't until we got back in the car that I finally said, "Thank you! For whatever this grand gesture is on my wrist." Jaxon told me there was no need to thank him. "This is officially my job, and I don't need other men looking at you thinking you need them." All I could do was laugh at Jax because it is super cute hearing him crush on me like this. The way he treats me makes me want to open up and begin a new journey with him. The distance scares me, though. For some reason, I felt a little sleepy, so I laid my head on Jaxon's shoulder. Maybe it's the blindfold. If you're in the dark, it is like you automatically get sleepy. "Talk to me." I said. He replied, "Sure, baby, what's on your mind?" I respond, "Life, can I be honest for a second?" I thought that's what we were doing, sweetheart. I started laughing then begin to explain to Jax how I felt about him. "I don't want things to end between us due to the distance, but I also don't want to move too quickly. Not because I'm scared, well, maybe I am. I just like you a lot and don't want anything to ruin our chances, you know?" Jaxon calmly responded, "I'm not going to let anything, not even distance come between us. I've already started falling for you, and it's too late to turn around now."

He grabbed my face gently and began to kiss me. I became so horny to the point my legs started shaking. Jaxon told the driver to pull in the nearest car garage and take a forty-five-minute break. I was confused when the driver opened his door and left, but not for long because next thing I know, I'm having hot, soul-melting sex in the back of a Rolls Royce. Jaxon started eating my pussy as soon as the driver closed the door. It's like I lost my soul for the second time as soon as I reached my climax, and it only got better. I was so turned on by the time we switched positions I had wet half the back seat. We spent the next forty-five minutes having passionate sexual intercourse that led to the losing of my blindfold and my panties. Things got so heated that we ended up outside the car on top of the hood. The feeling of it all gave me a rush. Jaxon made sure to kiss every inch of my body, including my toes every time we had sex. The looks we exchanged between strokes were priceless and breathtaking. I know we just met, but all I could see was love in his eyes.

When Jaxon finally nutted, he looked at me and asked, "Is there any way that I can convince you to stay with me?" I replied, "How about this, we start out slow, and in three to six months, we discuss moving in together." Jaxon smiled and hugged me before his phone began to ring, which made be suspicious because how many phones does he need? He gets dressed and starts having weird convos kind of, like the one he had on the ship. I keep hearing him speak of bricks. It may be his real estate license. I put my clothes back on, fixed my hair, and antici- pated our next adventure. When Jaxon and the driver got back in the car, he seemed upset, but I knew it wasn't with the driver. I asked him what was wrong with the driver. He replied, "Nothing… I can't handle, babe. I told you to stay stress -free. Nothing is going to ruin our day." I smiled and said, ok. "Where is your blindfold?" he asked. I looked at him and started shrugging my shoulders. That's the same thing I want to know. When you find it, let me know. "that ruins the surprises." Jax- on responded. I let him know that I would be fine without the blindfold because he never ceases to amaze me. "It's not like you told me where we would be going." You're right."Jaxon said. He instructed the driver to turn up the music and get us to our destination safely. The driver nodded his head at Jaxon and did as he was told.

We rode in the car for about an hour before we arrived at this grand fair. That's exactly what the sign read at the entrance, "The Grand Fair!" I honestly understood how it got its name. The fair was huge and full of exciting rides and booths. A person could go from the Ferris wheel to the food booths and even to the jewelry booth. There was so much to choose from, so when Jaxon asked what I wanted to do at first, I just smiled and started walking. For some reason, I wanted to hold Jaxon's hand, so I did. First, I went to the food booth, of course, to get a chicken on the stick and lemonade. When done with our food, Jaxon won me two big bears, and we got on the Ferris wheel. It was sweet and romantic. We spent most of our time talking, laughing, and getting to know more about each other. I learned a lot of information that I had been dying to know. Such as where his family was. It was odd at first because Jaxon was like, "You and my mom are going to get along great." I didn't expect him to say that. It made me feel as if I was about to meet her right there at the fair. He was just trying to let me know that his mom and I are similar in many ways. His father died when he was twelve, but his mother is still alive and lives an hour away. I'm supposed to meet her when I come back to visit. I'm nervous as fuck as if I'm meeting her today. He showed me family portraits, and I showed him pictures as well.

We rode a few rides and continued to flirt the day away as if Cupid kept shooting us with arrows. We left the fair after three great hours and went to dinner. Jaxon and I ate at the five-star restaurant called "El Leroy's." El Leroy's had everything from lobster to meatloaf. The menu was full of so many choices that I had to order a mixture of things. "Well, as our night comes to an end, I just want to let you know I've enjoyed your company." says Jaxon. "I enjoyed you as well Jaxon, thanks for being a gentleman." I replied. Surprised by the fact our driver was missing and so was the car, I asked, "Uh, where's our ride? Did we get dumped?" Jaxon started laughing hysterically then told me to turn around. Still no sight of the car. All I see is this angelic white carriage and four beautiful white horses. I continue to look past the carriage in search of the car. Jaxon is still laughing. For what exact reason? I don't know. He finally picks me up, and places me in the carriage and explains the joke. "The carriage is our ride, silly girl." Now I'm laughing uncontrollably because how in the fuck did I miss that? This man is taking my shoes off. What is the fucking catch? You rub my feet, make sure I eat, give me your undivided attention, etc..... He smiles and continues to rub my feet. "I guess you'll have to find out." Jaxon said. My fat full ass fell asleep on the ride home. That foot rub did it. When I woke up, he was carrying me into the house. "Is kids the catch, a crazy baby mama, or you're a slick dog?" I asked. "None of that man. You wake up joking around." Jax responded. "I do the things I do for you because I like you. I'm blessed enough to bless you and make sure you are beyond good, so that's what I'm going to do." He replied. "Thank you! I like you too, and appreciate you." I stated. "Now, where do you want to sleep? I had Maria renovate your room and readjust some things to ensure your comfort. I know you like and need privacy sometimes, but you always can sleep with me." Jax said. "I'll decide while I'm in the shower." I replied. When Jaxon laid me on my new bed, all I could do was cry, because it's like he listened to everything I said throughout the day and put it into my room. Jaxon hugged me and told me to stop crying before he stops buying gifts. That was funny considering the fact he gave me life in such a short period of time. I grabbed Jaxon's hand and led him to my new walk -in shower. We began to kiss and undress. Jaxon picked me up and sat me on the sink, then ate me like I was his last meal. When I reached my climax, Jaxon picked me up, turned the shower on, then began to slowly fuck me. It felt so good, and I almost told him I wasn't leaving anymore. The shower had a nice built -in bench that Jaxon bent me over on. He is so built, tall, and strong that my feet weren't even on the ground. I have never experienced any frog shit like that, but it felt sensational. I knew I was going to sleep like a baby. He must have known I was tired because he bathes me after we had sex. The man even moisturized my body with lotion and put me in bed. Jaxon held me all night, and I didn't mind at all. The things that usually annoy me was becoming comfortable for me. Things I usually wouldn't do with guys. I would do it for Jax.

I woke up to a full-body massage and breakfast in bed, of course. Jaxon was nowhere to be found when I finished breakfast, so I started to get dressed and prepare to depart. As soon as I put my shoes on and grabbed my last bag, Jaxon walks in and gives me a kiss and some keys. I gave the keys back and told him they weren't mine. Jaxon grabbed my bags and said, "Yes, they are. Come on." As I walk out the door, my knees become heavy, and so does my feet. "You still got the money I gave you on the boat, sweetheart? Never mind…, I put ten grand in your armrest, gassed you up, and put some snacks in a bag for you." Jaxon said. "Jaxon, I can't feel my feet. Did you buy me an all matte black Range Rover? How am I supposed to go home if you keep spoiling me?" I asked. "You are at home." Jaxon replied. "You are insured, and I mailed the official tag to your hometown." He explained. "It's funny how you said hometown, but anyway I'll call you, and don't have no bitch in my room. I'm going to miss you. Don't get funny." Jaxon laughed and gave me kisses and hugs. "No worries. I will come to see you in a week or two." Says Jaxon. I told him I would see him later, and to dream about me. I drove off feeling like I was leaving my husband to go perform duties in Iraq. I missed him before I even left his presence. As if we had been together forever.

CHAPTER 7:

Say Goodbye

During the drive home, Jaxon made sure to call me every two hours to check on me. Which only made it harder and harder for me to try and not fall for him. He does everything exactly how a girl would want it done. I dream of meeting men like him every day, and now I have finally met that man. Jaxon calls me right when I pull in my driveway. "You made it, baby?" He asked. "Yes, indeed, I'm getting my things out of the car as we speak. I'll call you as soon as I… *drops the phone and screams* I no longer could find words to talk. I couldn't even hear my neighbors come into the house because it was like my whole world had fallen in on me. I felt as if someone had ripped my heart right out of my chest and fed it to a tank full of sharks. Nothing could prepare me for the gruesome things I had just witnessed once inside my home. The house was a wreck as if someone forced themselves in through the side door. Broken glass, furniture, and pictures laid all over. That wasn't even the worst part. My father laid in the middle of the floor in a pool of blood, faced down. Bloody, life-less, and a stench as if he had been there for a couple of days. His throat was slit, hands and feet were tied, and mouth taped. He also had multiple stab wounds to his back as if he was attacked from behind. My ears went out, my mouth wouldn't move, and my legs felt as if cinder blocks were attached to them. This tragedy had put me in a coma-like state. I was trying my hardest to escape my thoughts, mind, and head altogether. I wanted so desperately to talk to the police and everyone else in the neighborhood who responded to my cry. Every time I opened my mouth, the only thing that came out was more cries and screams. I have now lost both of my parents, and I don't know where to even begin with this new heartache of mine. I don't know how to heal. I don't know how to continue life without the person who gave me a life. The pain was so unbearable that I fainted and woke up at the hospital. It felt as if I was reliving the same nightmare repeatedly. I would wake up in the bed at the hospital and slowly begin to panic. This is because every time I became conscious, I pictured my father lying in his own blood. This was a hard pill for me to swallow. The nurses and doctors kept me hospitalized and sedated until time for the funeral. The funeral home left me a letter saying that my father's funeral had been taken care of. They never stated how. They just let me know about the funeral arrangements and that they were handled. I didn't follow up and ask questions because I honestly didn't know how to talk about it. All I wanted to do was sleep the pain away. Friday morning, I woke up knowing that I needed to prepare myself for the funeral on Saturday morning.

As I open my eyes, I noticed a man sleeping on a sofa that wasn't in my room when I dozed off. I leaned up to see what the hell was going on, and Jaxon was sleeping like a baby. I felt so much comfort in seeing him there, but I also didn't know how to interact with him during my time of grief. I tried to pull myself together while he was still asleep, but I'm guessing he felt me or sensed I was up. The first thing he said was, "stop worrying, and get more rest. I'm not going anywhere until you are well." Jaxon insisted. I listened because I knew he was right. I went back to sleep for another four hours. Jaxon had filled my hospital room with five dozen of red roses. The flowers made me feel bright on the inside, but a part of me was still slowly deteriorating. He had also bought me a beautiful dress and made me an appointment for a full spa day. I appreciated those gestures and knew that from the look on Jaxon's face that he needed me to climb from underneath the dark rocks I was hiding under and put forth an effort to feel better. This spa day was to help Jaxon and me both. I had been too sad to even wonder about my friends, but seeing Jaxon here for me makes me angry that I haven't seen them. I really can't be mad though because I don't know if they came and I was asleep. Once I got dressed, Jaxon and I went to a spa called "Relaxation Station" He held my hand during each massage. I guess he wanted to reassure me that he was there. The back massage was so exhilarating that I drifted off to sleep naturally. That was the first time since my father died that I could fall asleep without being sedated. After a two-hour back massage, we got a forty-five-minute foot massage. Then we moved on to the facial station where we got full facials and face massages.

These enchanted creature's even massaged my arms and booty. They didn't miss a spot. I even got a manicure and pedicure. When they were done with me, I felt rejuvenated. I felt like a dying flower that begins to bloom again. I know this was only a start, but I was glad to feel a little better. I didn't mind being around Jaxon because instead of making awkward conversation, that leads up to a person repeatedly asking, "are you ok?" When knowing you are not. He would just grab my hand, kiss me, and hold me. No stupid questions, no extra stress, and no money problems because he handles everything. It's like this man is the African American superman. He swoops right in every time I need saving .The part that amazes me is I never have to ask nor tell him that I need help. He always makes it his job to solve my problems. After we left the spa, we went out to eat. Jaxon chose "Aunt Lulu's", a restaurant you'll find yourself standing up to eat in if you don't RSVP. Good thing Jaxon did reserve a table for two. The menu ranged from mac and cheese, rice and gravy, fried chicken, collard greens, dressing, potato salad, and so much more. Any food that puts the "s" in soul food is served at Aunt Lulu's. I ordered fried catfish, grits, and scrambled eggs from their brunch menu. Jaxon ordered smothered pork chops, rice and gravy, corn, and green beans. Safe to say, we left with a huge smile on our souls. The food was amazing and gave me the strength that the nasty hospital food couldn't. We also grabbed dessert to go. We had strawberry cheesecake and pound cake. We took it in after our nice meal. Jaxon paid for a two-bedroom condo by the beach. It was spacious, quiet, and comfy. He handed me the keys and the lease once we were inside. The lease was a six-month lease under my name. I told him to add his name and get a double key, but he insisted that he didn't need one. "You are moving into a new home near me or moving with me."

"This condo is a temporary clubhouse for my baby to recover at peace." I kissed him and thanked him. No need for me to argue against moving. I have nothing. I could leave today, and nothing else matters. "I'm giving you a six-month paid vacation. Lights, water, rent, and Wi-Fi is paid up for seven months. I'm only giving you six months before I carry you over my shoulders to our home." Jaxon stated. I laid in his arms and cried, but I assured him I would be ready. He went on to remind me how he told me that he would never allow me to drown myself in stress anymore. Then Jaxon ran me a bubble bath and bathed me like I was a wounded baby. Afterward, he held me until I fell asleep. I slept wonderfully, but as soon as I woke up, it felt like bricks were piling up inside my chest. I knew that today was the day. The day that I had to put the biggest panties of all on. I wanted my dad to rest in peace, so I just kept telling myself to pull it together and be strong. I felt strong, but my legs were weak. I didn't know how to make them move if that makes sense. The tears begin to roll down my face. I quickly wiped them and began to say a prayer. I knew Jaxon would come in with breakfast in a minute. I had to pull myself together. If I didn't pull myself together, I was going to be moving right after the funeral. I know Jax is going to scoop me up and fly away if I show one sign of stress. I'm not ready for that even though the people I love the most are dead. They both died in this city that I happen to love. I grew up here, and my friends still live here. Jaxon walked in shortly after I had begun to surround myself with deep depressing thoughts. I quickly came back to reality.

My legs started working and everything. Something about the smell of french toast, hash brown casserole, and ham and cheese omelets that'll wake the organs up. I admire everything about Jaxon. He's the only man that is consistent when it comes to me. He's always going to bring me breakfast that makes me want to get out of bed. Even though I was on the move, my legs and knees still felt like dead weight. I felt like I was trying to move mountains, when I was only swinging them back and forth from the side of the bed as I ate. Jaxon leaned in and kissed me before hopping in the shower. What a sweetheart. I quickly finished my breakfast, applied face wash, undressed, and joined him in the shower. Deep down inside, I wanted Jaxon to kiss me passionately, then make love to my body after his tongue kissed my vagina, of course. I couldn't say that, though. We had a funeral to attend if I didn't die before we got there. How could I even be thinking about sex at a time like this? I texted Brielle my new address. She wanted to ride with us to the funeral. As soon as we were getting out of the shower, Brielle comes knocking on the door. On -time, of course. She was carrying a dozen pink roses and two big blunts as if she was burying her father. I was so happy to see her and her marijuana. I knew that I would arrive at the funeral smelling loud, but at this point, I don't give a fuck. That weed is going to help me appear stable. When I asked Brielle to light the blunt, she began to laugh and cry simultaneously. I was confused. I never witnessed that in my life.

"Excuse me, Mr. Handsome, I didn't know you were here." I'm crying because I now know that you are going through something that is deeper than the surface. I knew it was a tough situation, but Anna, no matter what you go through, you never smoked nor drank your way through it. That's why I'm crying and laughing because all the time you complained about me smoking. Who would have ever thought you'd be taking a puff of your own? I have prayed for times like this." She explained. Brielle made me laugh so hard because she was right. I was hurting, and I hated to smell like smoke, but at this point, I don't give a fuck. I told Brielle to light the blunt. Let's put the past behind us because, at this point, I need her and that funky piece of happiness. She laughed even harder and lit the blunt. I gave her the biggest hug because I really missed her. She always comes late, but always on time. After we spent twenty-five minutes together laughing, crying, and smoking, my dumb ass finally thought to introduce my future baby daddy and my BFF. "I'm sorry, babe. This is one of my best friends, Brielle, and this is Jaxon." I explained. "Nice to meet you." They both reply. We loaded up in the limo shortly after. I felt stronger than ever with both Jax and Elle by my side. The ride to the church was silent and deadly. I had to ask the driver to pull over so that I could throw up. He parked at a nearby store where Jaxon went in and got napkins and a cold sprite to settle my stomach. I felt much better.

Thank God I'm still high, without the highness, I would be lower than low. Who wants to cry and vomit at the same time? That's like having a drunk cry baby on your hands. The herbs made me feel calm, but the thought of my dad in a casket still turned my stomach. Once the driver made sure we were back in safely, he drove us to, "Holy Mount Zion". That's the church we've attended ever since I was a baby. I didn't always attend like I should have, but my father was there faithfully. Everyone had formed a line at the door and waited for me to take my place at the front before walking in. Jaxon and Elle will walk in with me, of course. Pastor Fulton gave me a hug and said a prayer over me before starting the walk of heartbreak. I walked over and grabbed a piece of gum out of Jaxon's pockets and took the deepest breath that I could before I pushed the doors open. I walked into the church, and I saw the choir singing, clapping, and praising the Lord. I saw my father's casket, his work buddies, beautiful flowers, and a few pictures. I saw the drummer drumming, the praise dancers praising, but I heard nothing. The moment I walked through those doors, my ears went out. I didn't panic. I grabbed Jaxon's hand and continued to walk. As I approach the casket, I closed my eyes for ten seconds. I had to prepare my eyes for this last look at my father. I opened my eyes, and I was okay, my dad looked at peace. I looked down at his wrist because Jaxon bought him a nice Rolex to match his white and gold casket. When I came back to reality, the funeral was ending, and Jaxon was carrying me to the limo. He kissed me on the forehead and said, "We're about to go to the gravesite, then the repass. You need to eat." Says Jaxon. I just nodded and put my seatbelt on once he sat me in the limo. We buried him next to my mom, and then we ate at this beautiful place called, "Soul Landing." A catering company that takes your dinner, dates, and reunions serious. The company basically takes your ideas and makes them a reality. My dad loved to be outside, so Jaxon rented a big field and set up twenty big cabanas that had enough space to eat and lounge. Brielle told me that Kaylee couldn't make it because she was on the way back home from New York. I probably would see her tomorrow, and I'm not tripping. Jax also had these people bring a portable dance floor. He did everything that I know I wouldn't have been able to do in the state I was in. Soul Landing had everything! Lobster, shrimp, grilled & baked fish, mashed potatoes, dressing, chicken, pecan pie, greens, dumplings, green beans, macaroni, etc. They even had a bar cabana and dessert cabana. Kids had a choice of ice cream and pie or kettle corn and cotton candy. I didn't know if I was at the beach, fair, or grandma's kitchen. I must have still been high because my slim-fat ass ate everything that was on the menu. Summer was there. I didn't know she came until Elle pointed her out in the baked beans line. That's my friend. "Get in where you fit in!" had always been our motto. I introduced her to my boy toy. With his loving self. Summer immediately said, "Hey, mister, so when is the wedding and baby shower?" Jax chocked on his drink from laughter. He explained to Summer that he would be more than ready whenever I am. He then went on to ask Summer and Brielle how they'd feel about me moving with him. "Hot fucking damn boy! You got a brother, friend, cousin, or twin?" Summer asked. "Bae, I have to get another drink before Summer makes me waste all of mine." Jaxon explained. I laughed and grabbed my cell. I hadn't used it in a while. I hadn't posted on social media or anything.

So, I took a picture of Brielle, Summer and I under the cabana and posted it on Facebook. We all held endless convos as we danced on the floor. Jaxon made it feel like a celebration instead of a funeral after -party. The cleanup crew had the property back to normal in no time, so it didn't matter that we ate and danced until ten o'clock p.m. The scenery, decorations, and cabanas were so beautiful that strangers passing by started stopping and asking could they join the party. I didn't mind considering the fact we had plenty of food, and I didn't want to waste it. Thank God everyone ate and appeared to be happy. I did not have siblings, and now, I also didn't have parents. This made me appreciate the times like this when I'm surrounded by a room full of people. Well, a field in this case. I hadn't seen Jaxon in a while, but when he pulled up in the range, I felt better. I knew he had gone to get the car. I don't know; maybe I needed him in a way. It just feels good to know he is reliable. Summer drove, so she left the moment she saw people cleaning. Lazy ass best friend of mine. Jax and I dropped Elle off to her car, then rode to the beach. We took a long peaceful walk, then sat close to the water and talked as the waves came back and forth, rushing to shore like the lord was rocking the water like a baby. "I'm falling for you, and it's not a slow fall Anna. You make me want to do things that I have never desired to do. I am more than serious about us, and I am not going anywhere." Says Jaxon. I took the blanket that Jaxon brought out of the car and laid it out on top of the sand. "I just want to know you are safe 24/7." Jaxon continued as I undressed.

He turned around when I didn't respond and stopped everything he was saying. He slowly started to undress and walk towards me. I wanted to feel every kiss, every inch, and every piece of his chocolate body up against mine. I told him to lay down next to me and let me take control. I started off kissing his ears, then his lips then his neck. I wanted to make him as hard as possible. I ran my tongue down his chest and abdomen, slowly planting kisses all over his beautifully built body. When I got to his penis, he was hard as a brick and ready for the ride of his life. I began giving him fellatio, and I could tell he was enjoying every moment because he began to moan. The kind most men can hide if you don't listen. After about twenty-five minutes, I got off my knees and got on my feet. I squatted on his penis and rode him slowly to make sure he wouldn't nut after such intense head. Once he cooled down and got the hang of the ride, I spun around on the dick and went back to the knee work. I laid flat in between his legs and started riding him full speed backward. All he could do was grab my ass and moan until we both reached our climax. We took a nut nap afterward. A nut nap is a two-hour nap that helps you bounce back after you nut. Jax woke me up afterward and , carried me to the car. The condo wasn't far, but by the time we parked I had dozed off again, so of course he carried me from the car and put me back in the bed.

Although in my sleep, I heard him having another conversation about pounds and bricks. Unless I was dreaming. I was too sleepy to get the full scoop. Long as it wasn't a bitch. "Baby, please wake up, I can't leave without kissing and hugging you." Jaxon said as he shook me lightly around 5:30am. I woke up, and my boyfriend had his bags and all his belongings. The tables have turned, and I now understand how he felt when I had to leave. I hugged him so tight that we started laughing. "What's wrong with you, my sweet girlfriend? You never hugged me this tight I should be hugging you. You're the one that fucked me like a porn star. How am I supposed to live?" I started laughing as the tears rolled down my face. I couldn't talk while crying and I couldn't let him see my face, that's why I held him so tight. When I let go, I told him I loved him and that I was falling for him too. "I've just been hurt, Jaxon. That's why sometimes I can't speak about how I feel because I'm scared." I explained. "I understand, but you're mine now. I got you." Says Jaxon. I walked my new boyfriend to his ride, gave him kisses, and prayed he makes it home safe. We talked damn near the whole time he was on the road anyway. I told him I would call him once he got settled in. I know he had a lot of work to get back to considering the fact he had to take off to come to be with me. He said his goodbyes, and so did I. More like see you later rather than goodbye.

CHAPTER 8:

Time Tells All

Two months had gone by and there was still no new evidence or leads in my father's case. I started wondering if they were even still investigating. Time will tell. What's done in the dark always comes to light. God makes sure of that. Jax and I are doing better than ever. We took turns visiting each other until my six months were up. It was my turn to visit Jaxon, so I made sure to pack my bag on Thursday night so I could head out Friday after work. I had a new job as a desk clerk at a nearby hospital. I only made $9.50 an hour, but my hours and pay were good. I also got off early on Fridays and had Saturday thru Sunday off. Jaxon left that Sunday after my dad's funeral, and we prayed over the phone for God to bless me with a job. Well, I prayed. Jaxon touched and agreed because, honestly, he prefers, I drop everything and be a stay at home wife who doesn't face the harsh realities of life. I can't do that, though. Not at this moment. I'm trying to find a balance in my life and get it to feel like normal. Even though being without your parents isn't normal. I refuse to dwell on the past. I know my father would want me to continue my life like nothing happened. I woke up Friday morning to a lovely good morning text and three missed facetime calls. My man thinks that if he facetime me every morning, it'll make these six months go by faster. I don't have a clue why he's talking like he's in prison. I love waking up and going to sleep, knowing that I am loved. I kind of put us living together in the…, not to the back, but in the middle of my mind. I feel like I'm scared of that mark in the relationship that everyone reaches. The point when your man stops complimenting you on the things that you try so desperately to keep pretty for him.

The point when he stops blowing you up and starts telling his friends you're "bugging" him. The point when his homeboys become his girlfriends to cover up the fact that he's hanging with side bitches. When I say his homeboys become his girlfriends, you know exactly what I mean. They become his condom for every lie he tells, for every hoe he smells, for everything from hell. Because they're going to lie together, get high together, ride together, and die together. If they thought for a second, I was going for that shit. But the thing is, I have already been through that shit with one guy. I'm not doing that anymore. That shit is mind -blowing and chest wrecking. Your chest will collapse, trying to keep tabs on a no-good ass nigga. I need to shut the fuck up, though, because my man has done nothing wrong. My guard is just still up because of my previous relationships. I must let it all go though and move forward. I facetimed him back on the way to work. That nigga told me he wants me to get the cash he sent me out the mail and mail it to the return address since I can't answer when he is trying to make sure I'm ok.

I laughed and said, "I'm coming home today, daddy."

"That's what I like to hear." Jax replied. He said he had to get a lot of things to prepare for my arrival, so he blew kisses and hung up. That man is too handsome and adorable. He makes my soul melt and gives me butterflies. Work went by fast, which Friday's usually do. People hate visiting the doctor on the weekends. I spent five hours sitting at my desk looking for jobs near my boyfriend. I saw three desk positions at the hospital he worked at, but I prefer not to work at the same location as him. I don't want to seem pushy, clingy, nor needy. I don't want people all in our business because coworkers can be messy at times. When it comes to my check, I don't do messy nor "co-friends" Even though Jaxon is probably going to tell me that I don't need a job. I finally got a chance to stop thinking about it when I heard the gas pump automatically stop because my truck was full. I doubled back to my condo to check the mail. This man makes me want to move. What the fuck do I need five grand to travel eight hours to my man for? Jax is crazy sweet. I paid this company called, "secured secured" to put a built-in safe inside my tub.

Not because I'm hiding it from bae, but because I'm already extra straight. This money could add up to millions if we ever fall short and I need it. It's crazy how you can put a woman in a position to win, and in the end, she uses it to build a future that will forever be solid. A girl would blow the money on a bag but have nothing to put inside the bag. That's why I'm cautious of every move I make. When a man gives you everything you need and want, you have no choice but to level up and become a boss bae. If you don't, you'll soon become a broke bae. A broke bitch who is only seen as a piece of pussy. Broke baes never level up. They don't realize they're broke until their man levels up and leaves them. I called Jaxon soon as I got on the road, but he didn't answer. That's a first. I called Elle and Kaylee to let them know I was getting on the road and to catch up on gossip. Elle had just started a new job as a traveling makeup artist. She needed two-thousand dollars to start her team -up. I gave it to her because I have more than enough money. I am excited because she's doing weddings out of town and shit now. Clients must drop three bands as a deposit just to book her now. Well, for weddings, the deposits start at 3000. She didn't answer either, so I just texted her. Kaylee answered, but for some reason, she's been distant. We went to the spa a month ago, but I can tell something was bothering her. When I asked about her boo thing, she ignored me then changed the subject. I went with the flow because everyone is fighting some sort of battle in life, whether it be a dry pussy or diabetes. She kept the conversation down to a minimum. She only answered the questions I asked and repeated them when it got quiet on the phone. Oh well, she'll talk when she's ready. That's the type of person Kaylee is. She goes into a turtle shell when faced with problems. No one is ever aware of the problem until she's over it. I understood her, though. I lost my dad and didn't want to talk, eat, live, really nothing at all. I started to feel nauseous when I hung up with Kaylee, so I pulled over to throw up. I felt better afterward. Maybe it was something I ate. I got back on the road headed to heaven.

Jaxon texted me and said, Babe, I promise to call back. Put your seatbelt on and be safe. I love you!" I replied and told him I was on my way and that I loved him also. I felt good after three hours on the road. I stopped at a McDonalds along the highway and got a fresh berry salad with a water to drink. I didn't have a taste for anything greasy. I didn't want to make an 8 hour trip turn into a 12 hour trip due to bathroom stops. Jaxon still hadn't called me. I started to worry, but I thought to myself he's probably busy, or trying to buy me the world. When I already have that in him. It took me 7 and a half hours to arrive at Jaxon's house. I put the code in the keypad to the gate and let myself in. I knew the code and had my own keys, but I prayed I didn't enter and see some shit that's going to make me want to tear the house down. I put my key in the lock so slow that the maid walked past, doubled back, and opened the door for me.

I laughed and said, "Thanks!" "How are you, Anna?

Your key did not work? I'll go make you a spare." Lena said.

"No, thanks, Lena. I was just carrying a lot of stuff. Where's Jaxon?" I asked.

"He told me to run you a bubble bath, take you to the massage room, and make sure you don't worry because he's coming home."Lena explained.

"Thank you. I'll go ahead and take my bath if I could have a little bitty teenie weenie snack. I'm starving and feel like I'm going to vomit." I said. "I'm not supposed to give you food, but I'll bring you a light tray of food to your bubble bath session. Don't tell Jaxon. You know he likes to wine and dine with you." Lena said. I laughed and promised not to tell. My room was just like I left it except it was clean. My books was where I left them, except, they're organized. I didn't make it to the massage. The jacuzzi jets put me in just the right mood to relax, bathe, and nap until my man came home. Once I dried off, I got straight in my bed and went to sleep. I felt like I had slept for thirty minutes, but Lena said I was asleep for two hours and needed to get up. My baby was forty minutes away and wanted me dressed when he arrived. Which was kind of hard considering the fact I did work today, traveled eight hours and it was way pass my bedtime. Especially, considering how that bubble bath made me feel. Lena handed me a low-cut deep-V designer jumpsuit. The sides and back were cut out. The jumpsuit fits so good it made me feel like I gained ten or fifteen pounds. My stylist for the night was so quick. I had twenty-five spare minutes. My lazy ass laid down in the chair in the movie room and dozed off. Lena woke me up when he pulled up. I owe her so much. Jaxon was so happy to see my face when he walked through the door. He picked me up and gave me a million kisses. He had roses coming through the door, of course. Six dozen to be exact. All of them were white.

"To what do I owe the pleasure? What's the occasion? What's the celebration?" I asked.

He held me tight, kissed my forehead, then got on one knee. Me now resting on his knee, looking in his eyes for clues. "You make me happy, and I do nothing but smile when I'm with you. I want you forever. I know you can't put a price on true love, but I'll pay you a life for a life. So, what do you say? You wanna make it official and become my wife?" Jaxon asked. I started crying and nodding my head, yes. I hugged him super tight for five minutes before he could even put my ring on. He bought me a twenty-four-karat gold princess cut engagement ring where diamonds went down each side of the ring The crazy thing is that he also bought me a bracelet to match the ring with today's date on it. He had that much faith in me saying yes that he had my bracelet and my ring customized. He carried me to the car like he always does and even then, I stayed in his lap. I couldn't believe this shit. The driver kept looking at me and smiling. He knew I was in love and shocked . Jax kept kissing me and rubbing my hair as I stared at my ring. "Talk to me. How's your day been going?" Jaxon asked.

"Honestly, sweetheart, I can't complain about anything. My days have been great. Thank you for everything". I replied. He kissed me again and said, "you don't have to thank me for doing the things I'm supposed to do. Taking care of you is my job." He said. I got butterflies again like this is my first time meeting this man. I didn't even try to ponder my brain to guess where he was taking me. When we pulled up to this beautiful all -white farmhouse, and I thought if we were about to ride horses again. The land was huge. The farm sat on thirty acres. Jaxon loves horses, and I think I have a soft spot for them as well. From the time we stepped out of the car, we were treated with five-star treatment. They met us at the car with freshly squeezed lemonade. On the inside of the farmhouse, they had food, liquor, souvenirs, and all types of horse -shaped items on the outside, they offered carriage tours around the farm. We took the tour of course, and enjoyed each other's company.

We got off the carriage halfway through the ride, and because he wanted to walk. We came around two big weeping willow trees, and there was a romantic dinner for two. There were so many roses surrounding the table that I made Jax take his shoes off. I didn't want us to smush my flowers too bad. He laughed, but he took them off. A chef was waiting patiently underneath a cabana for us to sit so that he could serve us our meal. Champagne was on the ice, and I was no longer hungry. I was horny, hot and bothered, and I prayed my nipples weren't hard. It was getting dark and windy, so Jaxon had the workers to start a bonfire, and wrap lights around the cabana where we were seated. The trees also had beautiful white lights wrapped around them. The sight of this farm at night makes the daytime look like shit. All the horses were humble and walking around at peace. Nobody was there except Jax, the employees, and I. The chef made us lobster, steak, stuffed baked potatoes, and shrimp pasta. I was literally stuffed halfway through my plate but gained the space in my tummy to finish two plates. "I love a woman that loves to eat."Jax said. "She's beautiful, Jaxon." The chef said. "Thank you." Jax and I both replied. I am stuffed bae I don't know if I can make it home." I said. "I'll carry you before I leave you." Jaxon stated. I knew he would, but I told him I've wanted to talk to him about our future together after my six months. "What do we need to talk about? You're going to move here and live with me in our home." He explained.

I laughed and said, "Okay honey, I know that much, I've been looking for a job. Not that I'm trying to move asap. I just want to be prepared." Jaxon let me say all that without interrupting me. He waited until I was finished talking to say, "You're not working anywhere, so save all your energy for me." His face was so serious that I knew this wasn't a subject he wanted to discuss further. I just agreed and gave him a kiss. Jaxon honestly wanted the best for me. The carriage picked us up shortly after our conversation and took us back to the car. We had chocolate covered strawberries during our carriage ride back to the parking lot. I only ate two because I was already full as fuck. I dozed off on the way to Jaxon's house. He started shaking me to wake me up. I woke up slobbering and laughing because he never does that. He normally just carries me in the house. I guess he's getting tired of using his muscles. "That's why after these six months, you're not working anymore. That's why I send you two bands every other month and pay all your bills, so you won't be overworked and underpaid. I ordered a new movie for us to watch, but we can watch it tomorrow." I laughed and replied, "Shut up, Jax. You just want me at home all day." He laughed and said, "Damn right, now come on let's go to bed." We took a shower together then got in the bed. He knew I was tired. There were no irritating sex signals being thrown. He simply turned the fan on, adjusted the air, and cuddled me until I fell asleep. Nights like these are the ones I pray to God for. Most men want sex after everything. They take you to the movies, and they want ass. Take you out to eat, and they expect you to invite them over for a night cap. You tell them your period is on, and they ask for head instead. It's a never-ending cycle of dumb shit. Now that I have somebody that's trying, I'm happy. I woke up to a full body massage, of course. Sometimes, I wonder does Jax set the alarm or just naturally wake up before me.

"Bae?" "Yes, Anna? Good morning." Jax answered. "Good morning. Why aren't you married already? You're perfect." I said. "Honestly, it's always been hard for me to commit to any of the women I've met in the past. I've been straight financially for a while. Most of the women who approach me only approach me because they want what's in my pockets. I approached you. I came on to you because I saw a person who I wanted to get to know Before I met you, it was "smash on sight" and no hoe, you can't stay the night. I should have just told them, no, but they did come on to me, and I was single. I knew you were the wifey for me because I changed my number and my ways that same day, I met you." Jaxon responded. I turned over on my back and looked him in his eyes, and I could tell he was serious. "You make me happy, and I love you, Jax. I appreciate you telling me the truth. I love how you put my needs before yours and always make sure I'm smiling. You treat me like a queen, and that's why I'm able to submit and call you My King." He gave me kisses and then said, "Get up, so I can spoil you." We got things to do and a wedding to plan. "Jax, it's day two, and for some reason, I feel like you're more excited than me." This man smiled and ran us a bubble bath. I felt nauseous on my way to the bathroom, but it went away. Maybe I need to stop eating everything. The tub in Jaxon's bathroom was so big . It was like a kid's pool. We turned the jets on and relaxed for awhile. Lena brought us fruit cups and mini muffins. "Thanks Lena. You know Anna loves a snack." Jaxon and I laughed because this was true . I don't understand this. Jaxon ate his fruit then asked what I wanted to do today. I told him we could watch the movie he bought, but I was indecisive about what I wanted to do today. All I wanted was his undivided attention. "Today is Saturday, which means we have one more day together, sadly." I mentioned. "I don't even want to hear that shit. You're not leaving until Monday, and I'm going to come to spend two weeks with you on Wednesday. I'm ready to be under one roof. Can I pay you to quit your job and pretend they let you go with a raise? Paid vacation or some shit? Jaxon asked. I laughed, then jumped out of the tub to vomit. Thank God I made it to the toilet. Jaxon was standing over me, dripping bubbles and water, but I didn't mind because he was holding my hair. "You think it was the food?" Jax asked.

"No, I think you would feel bad as well if it was." I replied. "Is your period about to come on, Bae? Do you usually get nauseous around that time? Do I need to run and get you meds?" Jaxon asked.

I couldn't respond because all of Jaxon's questions led me to realize that my period didn't come last month and is yet to come this month. I needed to go to the store alone, but I had no clue how. My man is super protective and babies me. I knew what to do. "Bae, can you go get me some Tylenol, Imodium AD, and pads?" I asked. Jaxon said yes and instantly left. I waited until I saw him pull off, then I got in the

Benz because my truck was blocked in. I was nervous and scared as I drove at seventy-five mph, trying to get to the nearest dollar store. The dollar store was fifteen minutes away. I made it in six minutes. I bought six different types of pregnancy tests. I couldn't ask Jaxon to grab the pregnancy tests because, for one, we just got engaged and already need tests. He's super excited about the wedding, but I don't know if I'm pregnant. So, I don't need him getting excited about this too and holding me romantically hostage. I know him. If I'm pregnant, he'll get on one of his phones and start planning a joint baby shower/ or wedding. It'll be a grand celebration, and we aren't even sure yet. That's why I kept it to myself. The store wasn't busy, so I was able to get in and get straight out.

Jaxon made it home ten minutes after me. I was dressed and, in the kitchen, eating. "You feel better, bae? Your stomach doesn't hurt anymore? You want to stay in or out?" Jax asked. I told him I was feeling better and that I didn't mind going out. I also told him if I felt sick that I would let him know if I didn't feel better. "Thanks for getting the meds and pads for me, baby." I added. Jaxon hugged me, then got dressed, we were casually cute today. He asked me if I was okay from the time we left home to the time we arrived at the art museum. We saw so many inspiring paintings. It made me want to paint, and I knew I couldn't draw nor paint. Jaxon planted kissed on my hands as he admired each painting.

We had a picnic when we left the museum. Lena packed us fresh fruit, ham, turkey, roast beef sandwiches, and of course, beverages. We ate at a nearby park where we watched the birds swim across the pond. We fed the birds and ducks with the leftover food. We left at 6:30 p.m. and made it home around 6:50 p.m. Throughout the weekend, I noticed Jaxon spent a lot of time on both his phones. His flip phone a little more than his iPhone. So, while Jax was in the shower, I did some snooping. I didn't find anything in his room nor any of the guest bedrooms, but I did find a room that required a passcode for entry. I guess if you have the key, you don't need the code. I went to the key rack, and Jaxon's keyring did hold an extra key. I never paid attention until now. I heard the water coming to a stop, so I yell in the master bedroom, "Bae turn it back on, I'm about to join you." He turned the shower back on, and I hurried and grabbed the key and speed-walk to the door. I looked in each direction before inserting the key. I have no clue where Lena is. Fuck that this is my house too. I unlock the door, and it begins to slowly open on its own, and to my surprise, there lies loads, pounds, a room full of narcotics. Drugs were everywhere. All types of drugs. Things I've never even seen before. I quickly shut the door even though it moved about five mph. I heard footsteps, so I ran to the kitchen, put the keys back, and grabbed whipped cream.

Jaxon came out of the room, dripping water everywhere. His towel was wrapped around him, but I could picture everything. Jaxon laughed when he saw the whipped cream. It was a perfect cover -up. Jaxon didn't suspect anything. He took my clothes off in the kitchen, picked me up, and laid me on the top of the long marble island countertop. Jax allowed his towel to drop as he applied the whipped cream from my nipples down to my vagina. When done, he licked the cream out of my vagina! Making sure he got every taste. He pushed his tongue in and out as if it was a penis. It felt so good. He then fingered me slowly while he kissed my navel and sucked my nipples. How to make a bitch forget. Class was in session. Just when I thought I was about to get some dick, this man stuck ice between his teeth and started rubbing it up against my clit before sucking my pussy completely dry. Fuck the drugs! This sex is illegal. He kept trying to get me to lay flat. But my body was overwhelmed. I looked at the clock as Jaxon stood up and placed his penis inside of me. He ate my pussy, for I know one good hour straight. That's why I can't wake up after sex. I realized he didn't use a condom, which made me mad, but I didn't stop him. I was too worked up and ready. My hormones were rushing out of control. Lena walked in right when things were getting good. Jaxon just picked me up and fucked me all the way to his room. I couldn't sleep afterward, so I wrote him a note, packed my things, and got on the road. Too much was happening, and I wasn't ready to explain, argue, nor figure shit out. I might be pregnant by a doctor/

or criminal. I left at 4:30 a.m. and made it home around 11:50 a.m. Jaxon called as soon as I walked through the door. "Bae, I hate you had to leave due to work, I'm not going to be able to fly out for at least another two months." Jaxon said.

"No worries babe, I'll be back up before you come here," I replied as I stared at the pregnancy test that read positive.

CHAPTER 8 ½:

CheckMate

One month later my phone rang, but I didn't answer. The number wasn't saved, so I ignored it. Ten minutes later, the foreign number sends me a text message. It read, "911, call me as soon as possible." My stomach dropped to my toes. I hired a private investigator two weeks after my dad's funeral. I never told anyone because I know what Jax and my friends would say. They wouldn't want me trying to handle FBI work. I don't care, though. I needed to know, so I waited until I was alone to call back. HD is the private investigator's name. "Hey, HD. Let's meet." I said. "Say less. Same spot? I'll be there." He replied. We met at a private location. I didn't want to be seen in public with him in case the killer had eyes on me. HD told me to prepare myself for the items and pictures he found. "Be careful young one. Something fishy is going on. I hacked into the security system at your house, and whoever did this knew your family well. It wasn't a forced entry. The crime scene was staged. It had to be. The person who entered your home used the correct security code to disarm the alarm. The autopsy should tell you the time of death. If my allegations lead me right, this had to be done late at night or early in the morning. If the alarm had to be disarmed." HD explained.

"My dad always sets the alarm before bed and disarm it after work. He never forgets, so you're probably right." I responded.

"Even if this person studied your family's every move, they still would have had to be in the house before. How else would he or she know how to disarm the system? I don't know if you knew, but from inspecting the house, I found hidden cameras. I don't know if the killer planted them for his/her advantage or not. Your dad may have bought them for protection. Either way, the story must be on these cameras. I found a guy and girl sniffing around the crime scene. I took plenty of pictures because they seemed suspicious, but maybe I was just overreacting." He explained.

"Thank you so much HD. I appreciate you for all of your help." I replied. "No problem. I'll be done with all the cameras today. We can watch it together if you're scared." He insisted. "You can email it to me so I can watch it online. I can also open the envelope while watching." I responded. We went our separate ways after I paid him a thousand dollars more to look further into the female and male. I went back to work and pretended the envelope wasn't causing me an anxiety attack. We became super busy at work, which sort of took my mind off things. This muffin top was causing me to move slow, which made me extra busy. My next check -up was after work, but I rescheduled. I didn't feel like being bothered after working and investigating. As if I was helping HD in the field. Naptime and a bubble bath were calling my name. I ordered a pizza for delivery on the way home. I didn't plan on leaving the house once I made it.

The pizza arrived at the same time as the flower man. Jax had sent me flowers. Strange, though, because Jax doesn't use this certain flower company. Call me crazy, but I know my man. Jaxon always orders from a florist called, "Rose Garden." These flowers came from, "Flower Gallery." Plus, they weren't even roses. I ignored the signs, though. It's the thought that counts. I took a bath, ate some pizza, and had one glass of wine. The doctor approved of one glass a day. Pregnant women don't have to be completely miserable. I still haven't told Jaxon, because I plan on surprising him. He would have me on bed rest if he knew. Next month I'm going to surprise him. I'll be four months, and my bump will be showing for sure. I will be traveling to visit him, but he doesn't know that we will be going on a surprise trip to the gynecologist. I scheduled an ultrasound appointment so that he could find out and see his daughter or son. This way, he won't have to travel and miss work. He always surprises me, so I planned one of my own. I was super, nervous, and happy all at the same time. Because it has been 1 month since we seen one another and I really didn't know how to tell him because my very first appointment, the doctor told me I was two months pregnant going on three. I'm guessing that's where the weight gain was coming from. Despite my findings behind the secret locked door. I texted Jax to say thanks for my flowers. Of course, he would facetime back instead of texting. "Hey, bae. What flowers?" He asked. "Stop playing crazy. I know you sent me these flowers." I responded. "What nigga is crushing on you? Show me the flowers." He insisted. I walk in the kitchen blushing from head to toe because he's so sweet. Trying to act like he didn't send the flowers. I flip the camera to show him. "Bae, why are your feet swollen? Read the card to me so I can find the sender." He said.

I completely ignored him about the swollen feet and focused the camera somewhere else. As I opened the card, I begin to feel fear. I've felt what it was to be scared. I fear snakes, but I have never felt fear. I was in fear for my life. Tears rolled down my face because it was a bloody card. The card read, "Mind your business before you meet your dad in hell. Unless you want to end your bloodline before it starts well." Blood was literally all over my hand, the card, and the petals that lie beneath my hands. A soon as I opened it, blood dripped out. Enough blood to come from a minor cut, but not enough blood to destroys the message on the card. I forgot Jax was on facetime because I dropped my phone when I saw the blood. He was calling my name repeatedly, and when I didn't answer, he said he was on his way. "Talk to me sweetheart. Let me know something." He screamed. By the time I picked the phone up to lie, he hung up. I called HD, but he didn't answer. I called Jaxon back on the phone that does not have facetime. I couldn't let him see me upset. Tears were falling, and I looked like a wounded puppy. I needed to talk to him and tell the truth, considering the fact this coward threatened our unborn child. "Anna, what the fuck did that card say? I am packing now." Jaxon said as he answered the phone.

"I'm good, bae. I forgot Summer's birthday, and she sent flowers as a prank because I didn't get her anything. I buy her flowers every year for her birthday." I explained. A part of me knew he wasn't buying my lies.

"Oh, ok, sweetheart, I love you." He said. He has never gotten off the phone that fast. All I could do was pray; he believed me. HD offered to let me watch the hidden camera footage with him, but I declined. Thank God he wrote an address down in case I changed my mind. I got dressed in hopes of finding HD at this address. The GPS said the destination was thirty minutes away. I texted Jax so he wouldn't become antsy. He was acting weird, but he probably said the same thing about me. I spot HD's car in the yard, and a light is on inside of the trailer. I get out and grab my purse, the envelope, and I put my small handgun Jaxon bought me inside my purse. You can never be too safe. I didn't learn that until my father got killed. Jaxon bought it for me once he realized I felt unsafe but wasn't leaving my city because of it. Once I got out of the car, I knocked on the door hard as fuck because I didn't want to disturb him, but I was disturbed. I wait four minutes before knocking again.

The trailer was a nice size, but there is no way he didn't hear me. After my fourth time knocking, I grew impatient, so I twisted the doorknob, and the door is locked. I walk around the trailer, knocking on the windows until I get to the back, and the door is wide open. I walked slowly because I have had enough encounters with surprises to last me a lifetime. The trailer is quiet. Not a tv, radio, nor anybody talking. This makes going past the door creepy. You always feel when something bad is going on. I entered the trailer, and it looks just like my dad's murder. Blood and important items were everywhere. It looked like forced entry, but I didn't see HD. This made me even more scared. I began to think HD set me up to come here so he could kill me. I instantly start looking for the hidden footage. I looked through drawers, laptops, cabinets, and under the sofas. It wasn't until I went towards the rooms that I noticed the bloody footprints. I crept down the hallway while fishing for my gun inside of this treasure box ass purse. I come around the corner like a scared rookie cop pointing my gun as if it was in control. I turn the lights on, and the bloody guy is HD. He made it to the bed.

I run over to him and start to shake him, but the blood just gushed out of his wounds. I threw up all over the floor. When strong enough, I cleaned my face and started to search his bags and nightstands. My phone vibrates, it's Jaxon. He asked if I was asleep. I told him no, and he asked if I was I already in bed. I replied and told him yes, and that I may be asleep in a few minutes.

He read my message, but never texted me back. I put my phone in my purse, and HD grabs my arm and calls my name. I explain to him the importance of letting me know who did this. All he could say was, "Pocket vid." I shake him, but it was too late, he was gone. I checked his pockets, and there's nothing there, but a big ass hole. The right pocket consisted of four flash drives taped to his leg. I instantly grabbed everything I own plus the flash drives and ran to my truck. I couldn't watch until I was home, so the ride was very miserable for me. I am about ten minutes away from home when I notice an unfamiliar car following me. It was a white jeep wrangler. The driver falls back every other minute but makes every turn that I make. When I made it to the security gate, I use my gate button to access the side entrance. The front is for people who have a code instead of a key, basically for visitors. The fact that the jeep goes through the front tells me that they are visiting, or forgot their key. I got behind the jeep once it entered. I turned my lights off and proceeded to follow it. The motherfucker had the audacity to park in my parking spot next to my building. I waited for the man to get out because I saw a fade and out comes Jaxon. What in the living fuck? I instantly parked, then sat hesitantly because the last time we talked he was at his house and I was in bed, I can't question him because I'm supposed to be in bed. Then on top of that, I am pregnant. Three months to be exact. I'm not big, but I am not little like I used to be. I got out of the car and walked so slow to avoid talking to him. Jaxon came outside and grabbed my hand.

He said, "Speed up baby, because you have a lot of explaining to do." I started to chuckle, but then, I remembered everything and knew that I had to be honest about it. Including the bloodstains on my clothing, and the flash drives. Once we were in the house, Jax started drinking Henny and looking at me for answers. "Bae, can I shower first?" I asked. "We can talk while you shower." Jaxon replied. I agreed because I was tired of lying and I was scared. I took my clothes off and got in the shower. Jaxon came in shortly after me. He leaned up against the sink and continued to drink Henny. As the soap came to a lather. I told Jaxon everything about HD, and his findings, about the flowers and the card. After feeling like I aired everything out, Jaxon showed me I didn't. When I got out of the shower, he handed me a towel, kissed me, then threw all the pregnancy tests at me. "I'm hurt that you are still lying to me." Jaxon said. "I wanted to surprise you next month. I would be four months next month, and my tummy would be bigger. There's no reason for you to be upset. The baby is yours; we are going to be parents." I responded as I got dressed.

I looked up, and Jaxon is wiping tears from his eyes. "I'm not mad at you. I'm happy as fuck. Well, not mad anymore. I had a girlfriend cheat on me and get pregnant once before, so I apologize for throwing the tests. I was upset, but wrong. Let's just agree to be honest with one another. We both hate lies." Jax said. I apologized and agreed to keep everything out on the table. He gave me lots of kisses and told me he didn't want to lose me. I reminded him that he wouldn't. Jaxon got in the shower, and I heard him talking on the phone, but the water made it too hard for me to hear. I felt like he was using the water to block my hearing. Fuck it. I'll watch these videos and get a head start on who killed my dad. "Lord, please be with me and watch over my child, and not let stress affect his or her birth. Amen." I stopped praying after I inserted the flash drive, then began to pray again. "Lord, I thank you! You're always here with me. Father God, guide me throughout this video." I prayed. I decided to just press play. They weren't labeled, so I randomly picked. The first one I choose is of HD, talking to me. Guessing earlier today because he is wearing the same thing.

"Hey Anna, in the video there's a guy, and a girl who speak of you heavily, and a hitman was following me as I followed the guy and the girl. They were fucking on the balcony of their hotel, I waited, and they came out and I followed them to a pizza shop. When I got to the red light, the hitman got out and walked to my car. It was then that I recognized him from the security cameras at your dad's house. HD said. Someone pulled up. I couldn't see because HD stopped in his tracks and started hiding and packing shit up. I could hear him scream, "It's him, Anna." I took that one out and inserted the one inside of my envelope. It starts after my dad dies; I can tell how the house was. I know HD said we had unwanted visitors, but this footage seems blank. Right when I reached to take it out, in walks two visitors. They look familiar but haven't faced the camera for me to know for sure. Strangely these two know my house very well. They went through all the right cabinets when looking for wine glasses. They grabbed cover from the closet container. Normally, people go through at least four cabinets before guessing the right one. Lots of different closets to find blankets. My dad was neat, so he kept the remotes in a pull-out cubby under the entertainment center. These bitches even went to that without having to search. HD was right; they knew us. The shower stopped, and I heard a bitch voice, but my eyes are stuck on this bum bitch inside my house, eating, drinking, and fucking like she lives there. It wasn't until they got naked that I could identify them both. Their tattoos gave them away. I hurried and pulled the pictures out of the envelope while praying my eyes were lying to me. There lie Jason and Kaylee, plain as day, holding hands and walking through my door in the same clothing as the visitors in the videos. They appeared to be a couple. I understand why Jason is mad. He knows I kicked his ass along with his ego, but I can't seem to figure out why Kaylee did any of this. I now know why she's been distant and funny acting. The bitch is a wolf in sheep's clothing. A snake in disguise. I took the flash drive out and replaced it with another in anger and disgust.

This time, my stomach dropped because my dad is on the screen. Alive, well, and happy looking. He's watching tv, but something happens at the door. Instead of opening it strangely, he goes back and comes back with a gift. Kaylee enters the house and disarms the system. My dad looked confused and hugged Kaylee and proceeded to tell her I wasn't home. He thought she was me. This bitch looked my dad in his eyes and said, "She's coming through the back. She wanted to surprise you." He laughed, then went to the back door where he let the hitman in. He instantly started to kill my dad. Blood flew everywhere. This bitch let Jason through the front door while my dad opened the back. They all had gloves, meaning they were prepared to alter the crime scene with no worries. It hurt that my close friend could attempt such malicious acts and practically walked around free. This stupid ass bitch ate from the same plate as me. I never treated her any type of way. I was so mad that all I could do was think about my baby. Who would teach my daughter to get through her cycle if I was to shoot this hoe and sit behind bars? Not that I know the gender, but hypothetically speaking. I didn't know how to go to the cops without looking like I killed HD. So I decided to play everything cool until I gave birth to my child. I knew in the back of my mind that I was going to make them bitches suffer. I just had to figure out the best way to do it without going to jail. There is no way in hell I can give them the satisfaction of walking around breathing the same air as me, when they did what they did to my father. "Anna, I am not doing this anymore. Hand me the evidence on this case. This is no longer your problem, it's mine. I know you're hurt, but I got you. Get on my back. I need my babies safe. Live for me, and I'll stress for you." Jax said. I gave him everything, but I'll keep the video of them entering and committing the crime. I must show Summer and Elle. I don't want them to end up hurt. I don't even know who Kaylee is anymore. She always hated Jason. They couldn't beat me alone, so they linked up. Three minutes into the video of the murder, Jaxon starts punching and destroying my laptop. Why didn't I react like that? He started pacing and rubbing his head. "Go put your comfiest pajamas on, get all of your necessities, your charger, laptop, bonnet, and sneaks if you want. I already packed most of your stuff." Jaxon said.

Confused, horny, and scared because my man was speaking to me in a way that I knew he meant business. I was mainly scared because I knew Jaxon was mad. I have never truly seen him this way before. I ran to my closet, and my boxes were lined up neatly. Not a hanging hanger or skirt swinging This man really sat here and packed everything, but my comfy pajamas, purse, and bonnet. Jaxon loads the boxes in the car while I slide my travel pajamas on. He stop in his tracks when I start to empty our safe. "Damn bae, that looks like yacht money. Want to sail away? I told you that you were the wife for me. I can trust you if things ever go left. I really do love you, sweetheart. You don't have anything to grab at all if you don't want to. This will always be our condo when we visit. I dropped ten money orders in the dropbox, changed the locks, and added cameras. We are good, sweetheart, I promise. This won't be our permanent home. And bae, grab my laptop out of my bag when we get in the car so you can email that weak ass job and quit." Jaxon said. I am so blessed to call him my fiancé. I took everything, but twenty grand. I no longer wanted to fight to stay in this stupid ass city. "I paid some movers to move the rest of your things next week. I put the most important boxes in the back. If I forgot something important, I'll buy it first thing tomorrow." Jaxon said.

I told him not to worry about it because I was a free woman now, and I could go to the store whenever. I really don't want to get too bored with this not working thing. "Your feet are swollen, so what you can do is get a spa treatment, bed rest, and many reclined nights in the movie room." Jaxon said. I opened my snacks and adjusted my chair for the ride home. Eight long hours. Jaxon must have sobered up because, after my snack, I dozed off and only slightly woke up when Jaxon rubbed my tummy. Normally, he'll swerve at least two times and wake me up, or speed at uncomfortable speeds that wake me up. I dozed off, and next thing I know, Jaxon is tapping me. "Wake up, Lena just made breakfast. I'll make sure to put your things in our room and not your woman cave across the hall." Jax said. I kissed him and said, "Good! I'm ready to annoy you. I missed you." "Well, give daddy some sugar." Jax said while squeezing my ass. I ate my breakfast, then went to lie down. Jaxon had bought us a memory foam California king -sized bed. He also made everything unisex instead of masculine. My closet was still in another room, but I loved the space. I love this man. If I say my back aches, he buys a bed to accommodate me. I tell him something once, and I never have to repeat myself. My body melts into the bed as I relax Jaxon slides my panties down and starts eating my pussy. This man knows that my hormones are raging. It felt so amazing that I fell asleep and wasn't even aware of it. This baby is really draining me. Jaxon didn't mind, though as long as I wasn't stressed out.

CHAPTER 9:

End Game

Two months later…. It's cold as fuck in here, babies crying, mommy's lying, and so many people. "I love being pregnant." Says one mom. "My baby hardly cries. I don't know why she's so fussy today?" Another mom says. First of all I feel like I am carrying a basket on the front of me and a building on my back. I am dreading these tests and the needles. Today, Jax and I have an appointment for a 3D ultrasound. I am excited, but still very aggravated. Jax reads through the frustration on my face and grabs my hand. "You always get annoyed in the waiting room, It's almost our turn." He said before the nurse stepped through the door and called my name. "Annabella West." Even though it had been a month since we even got married. The wedding was approximately eleven months away, which kind of made it hard for me to remember that my last name was West. It'll all sink in soon enough. In the meantime, I piss in the cup, got my blood drawn, and wait on the doctor. Jaxon is so supportive that I almost felt like he's a better parent than me. Dr. Boa knocks on the door, then enters the room. He makes general conversation while washing his hands and applying his gloves. He calls the nurse when ready, and I closed my eyes and relaxed as he applied the warm gel to my itchy belly. I was okay until Jaxon dropped both his phones, and Dr. Boa dropped the gel. I opened my eyes, and there were two babies on the screen. I fainted, then woke up and said, "Jaxon, what happened?" He replied, "This happened." Then, he showed me the 3D ultrasound of two babies. I didn't say anything. Jaxon looked extremely happy. I'll wait until we're home to cry. That way, he won't see me. I can't cry in the car. "Babe, our family is complete, we have twins. A boy and a girl. You fainted before Dr. Boa could tell you." I nodded yes, and let my seat back to take a nap. I secretly hated them, both babies at this point. I know I'll love them later, but today, I'm mad.

Jaxon kept that stupid -ass smile on his face the whole night. Then he wanted to shop online and pick names. I started to say, Nigga, pick my casket because I must be dead. This isn't real life. I love that he's involved, but how do I prepare myself for two babies? "I'm here, and besides, the devil took two important people from you, your mother and father. Then, God blesses us with two important babies. Living, growing, and becoming great through you. You can hire a second Lena until the twins turn one years old. My main reason for saying until they are one is that I don't trust people around my kids. Lena can move into her bedroom upstairs. The new lady can come at 9am until 5:30pm. That'll give Lena a break time. We can do interviews in the Seventh month closer to the time of their arrival, maybe next month when you're seven months pregnant. We don't have much longer you'll be six month in a day or so. Right now we have to plan a baby shower, wedding, and names.." Jax said, "Sounds like you have everything planned out, but that sounds excellent, babe. Thank You!" I said. We ate dinner at home. I cooked fish, shrimp, and grits. Jaxon never had fish and grits together. So, I made it for us. My grandma used to always make it for me. I gave Lena a paid night off. She was as sweet as pie, and I honestly appreciated her. Jax and I had the house to ourselves, so it was a panties and too little t-shirt type of night. We ate in the movie theatre and watched Titanic. Jaxon has never seen it, and I love that movie. Of course, I cried during the movie. Jaxon made cookies and brownies over ice cream. I was like a kid in a candy store. I was never going to lose this fat ass baby weight. I honestly had zero complaints. Jaxon treats me phenomenal. I guess I spoke too soon because an unsaved number that I knew texted Jaxon's phone. I picked my phone up and typed the number in and it's Kaylee's number. Why the fuck is Kaylee texting my man. I must know what it says. I opened the message, and it's a picture of Kaylee from her phone, but she's dead. Gunshot wound to the head and chest. Another picture comes through, and It's Jason, dead as well. I scrolled to see if the person sent anything else. To my surprise, there's a thread of Jaxon and Kaylee arguing. She sent a screenshot of Jax and I. A picture that he must have taken because I have never seen the picture. Kaylee said, "This bitch must have been the reason you can't answer or be with me. Crazy how you're fucking my best friend. Both of y'all bitches are going to suffer." Jaxon replied, "Bitch, I hit you and quit you simply because you were easy. I never hit you back after that. That has nothing to do with my girlfriend. I didn't even know where you were from. Bitch, I didn't even know your name, but I know your face. Play pussy, and get fucked.Your pussy wasn't even good, neither was your personality. Bitch, BYE!" She never replied, but I never knew. What happened to being real? Why the fuck would a female who has known me forever kill my dad over a nigga? Not like I don't love him, but I loved her and never did anything malicious to her. Why would my husband hide a piece of information like this from me? I walked to the kitchen, and Jaxon was putting the left-over cookies in the fridge. Tell me about Kaylee. He asked who Kaylee was. "My best friend that teamed up with my ex to kill my father." I replied. "Listen, I never knew her name. I never even knew where she was from. Hell, I didn't even know she was your best friend." Jaxon answered. "That may be true, Jaxon, but I'm sure you knew she was a girl you fucked once you watched the video. That's the reason you got so mad after watching it. I thought you were mad because of what happened, but you were mad because you fucked the bitch involved, and now, you feel responsible." I added. "Anna, I was mad about both situations.

Of course, I felt responsible, but I fucked that hoe three months before meeting you. I was ignoring her way before I met you. You have to understand that I didn't know." Jaxon pleaded. The thing is, he never once mentioned he knew her after everything happened. That's the part that just isn't sitting well with me. He tried to hug me, but I pushed him away. "Anna, how does a man look his woman in the eyes and tell her that her dad is probably dead because of the love that we share it doesn't even sound right. Hey your dad is dead because I had a one night stand and now a hoe is mad because I love you and not her ?

How am I supposed to worry you when you already have an overload of stress that seems to be tearing at your body? The body that's carrying our future. How was I supposed to do that? All I knew was that I could handle the situation. I could never continue my life with you knowing a bitch hurt you and got the chance to live her life peacefully. Even if you were to leave me, I was still going to put money on their heads. I love you too much to allow anybody to slide with disrespecting you. If the lady at the nail shop breaks your nail, she's dead. That's just how I feel. You can be mad at me if you want. I'll sleep on the couch and all. Just don't leave me. Don't cause stress on the babies. I can't tell you about the illegal actions I take against people. It's for your safety. If shit ever gets rough for us, I want you to know you and the twins are good forever. I love you, Anna." Jaxon explained. I told him I love him too, and he wiped my tears. He asked if he really had to sleep on the couch. "No, the couch is not too comfy, but if you lie to me again, you will be sleeping on a twin-size air mattress at the foot of the bed. I'm so serious too, Jaxon." I said. He laughed, then helped me to bed. As we lay in bed playing footsies, I roll over to kiss Jax because I never said thank you. He kissed my lips, then forehead, then scoots down and lies on my stomach. As if the twins don't already have me weighed down. I felt like I was carrying twin bags of bricks, but I love how much he loves them already. Jax was on his phone, staring at a picture on social media. It would take me breaking my eyes to verify which one. "Who is the woman, bae?" I asked. He showed me the picture that was so beautiful and natural. It was off guard, and I was sleeping. I asked him when was the picture was taken? He took the picture two months after we met. He explained the significance of the picture. He said he wanted more than facetime calls. He needed memories to use when I wasn't in his presence. "Honestly, this is most likely the picture that made Kaylee angry. I posted it on social media not for her, but for every female who had eyes on me. I wanted them to know where my heart was." He responded.

I have never been so ready to say, "I do" in my life. I usually have doubts about getting married due to past relationships, but I am genuinely happy now. I look forward to being a mother and a wife. I know I am already both, but I guess I'm ready to re-marry him all over again. I know that Jaxon is the man for me. I know that he wouldn't hurt me in any way. He goes above and beyond for me and our children. I never wanted him for his money. I wanted him because he made me feel embarrassed for putting up with all the bullshit I settled for in the past. You removed the blindfold from my eyes, so I could discover my worth. Before I met him, I was blind. We said our prayers, kissed, and went to bed. I woke up the next morning feeling like a zombie. I didn't have any energy. Jaxon made the bed with me in it, so now, I'm extra comfy. I texted Lena for some pizza, and she woke me up to pizza on a platter in bed. Of course, my fat ass ate in bed, then shortly after fell back asleep. It was three hours past my wake up time and I still was laying in bed. I am going to get up and go shopping. I'll have to grab a shot of coffee or something. The crazy thing is, I haven't seen my husband since last night. He didn't even wake me when making the bed. I hope I haven't lost my opportunity to sneak out. I got out of bed quietly and start to tip-toe to my closet. As soon as I got close to the door, I saw a man with a ski mask through the mirror. He isn't looking my way. I close the door slowly, made my side of the bed, and grabbed my phone. I go into the bathroom then, through the secret door inside Jaxon's closet. It's a mini safe room. It's the smallest one in the fucking house. I thanked God there are snacks in here. It's soundproof, that's another reason I never heard Jaxon's conversations. I texted Lena to tell her to get to the safe. She never texted back. I texted Jaxon and told him. This bitch said, "You better be in one of the safe rooms. Fuck Lena. Don't try to save her. Save my children. There's a handprint on the wall that matches yours and one that matches mine. For snacks use yours, and for weapons place your hand in the middle of the handprint that matches mine. I'm on my way. Don't move Anna, please." Jaxon said. I heard a woman talking, and she sounded like Lena, but I'm not sure because this safe makes it hard to confirm there's a little speaker inside that allows you to hear outside of the room, but I had it on the lowest volume. "What the fuck do you mean she left? How? The window is up, but the vehicles are still parked out front." A woman says. A male voice replies, "You work here every fucking day. How the fuck did you choose today to lose her? How are we supposed to rob your boss if you don't know the code to the safe? You don't know where the safe is located, the code, or where either of your bosses is! You're just about the dumbest thief I have ever met." The male voice was deep and unfamiliar, but I confirmed that Lena was the culprit. I texted Jaxon to make sure they couldn't hear me. He said they couldn't. I told him it was Lena. Before I could send another text, bullets were sounding off. I didn't know who was shooting, nor who was in the room. Shots rang out in the bedroom or close to it. This went on for about six minutes straight. The twins were kicking uncontrollably. How can they cause their mommy pain at a time like this? I heard footsteps coming toward me. I sat there as still as a deer in headlights. The steps became louder, which means they are close as fuck. I prayed to God it's Jaxon. I heard the code being entered, and I started to pray harder. I closed my eyes and held the gun as tight as I could. I heard laughter once the door opened. "How were you going to shoot with your eyes closed?" Jaxon asked. I climbed out, and my bathroom and room were full of cops. Jaxon kissed me and thanked the chief of police for shooting and capturing the male. Lena was out of it. Jaxon had one of the officers lay her in her bed. I wasn't sure why. I was guessing he wants to torture her. I hope he doesn't kill her. When the officers left, Jaxon told me that he and the chief had been friends for twelve years. Now that I think about it, I have seen him out of uniform. He and Jaxon are always spending time together in that drug room that he keeps locked. I went to the bathroom, and someone rung the doorbell. "You are back, chief?" He asked. "Yea. I couldn't talk with all those clowns around me. You got a sec?" Chief asked. Jaxon replied yes and told him to come to his office. I hurried up and urinated so I can ear hustle. I leaned up against the wall, two inches away from the cracked door. I heard the chief say, "I got a drug bust going down tomorrow. Tyquan and his boys are the targets. They're making too much noise. Plus, the whole D.A. office is after them. You know they are liable to have thirty-million dollars worth of narcotics. All types of work. If that's the case, you know twenty-million of that is ours. Split the profit 50/50." Chief states.

Jaxon asked, "where does the other ten million go.?" The chief said, "That will go to the news as police findings. We can't get greedy. I've had eyes on Ty for about two months. The dude is moving hella work. Thirty million is just me guessing how much we'll find. It may be more." The chief explains. "Okay, listen. I'm straight as fuck. You're straight as fuck. I'll do this one last job with you under one condition." Jax said. "What's the condition? You are getting half?" he asked. Jaxon replied, "Don't misunderstand me when I say conditions. I'll move this work for both of us off the strength of how solid we are. The money is not a problem. After this, I'm done with it. This shit is worse than having a side bitch. I have never loved a whore. Never. So, when it's time for me to live my life as a doctor and father, that's exactly what I'm going to do. Oh, and plus a wonderful husband. Street money doesn't have insurance. I need to build a stable, settled empire for my wife and children. I don't mind dying if that means I can make sure they're straight. I have that opportunity. I love Anna, and she deserves a better me. I know I can give it to her. I just want you to understand we had a good run, and we did what we said we would." Jax said. "What was that, Jax?" "We paved a better way for our families, paid bills off, built a solid team, and made enough money to leave this shit better than when we came in. What the fuck you crying for?" Jaxon asked. "Shit, honestly, I'm happy for you and understand that I'm high. I love you, boy! I'll accept under one condition." Chief said.

Jaxon asked him what, and the chief said, "I want to be the God-father." Jaxon agreed, and they both began to walk out of the room. When Jaxon let the chief out, I asked him to grab me a bottle of water. I thought this would buy me some time to calm down. All this spying and running has me feeling like a track star, who happens to smoke ten blunts a day. Jaxon got to the room, and my big fat ass was still breathing hard as fuck. "Bae, what's wrong?" Jaxon asked. I lied and said that I was jogging to try to get some exercise in. It's good for the babies. "Whatever, how do you feel about moving after you have the twins?

Or do you want to move tomorrow?" Jaxon asked. "Fuck all that, did you handle Lena, the liar? I don't want her working anywhere near my kids." I said. "Anna, I hired Summer and Elle. That's probably why Lena tried to plan to rob me because she felt like she was about to be fired and homeless. They're going to move in with us once we move. I gave them enough money to quit their jobs a month before your due date and come out here. The choice is theirs. They said yes, though. Elle said she'll just start promoting her business in whatever area we move to. I assured her that her room would have space for makeup clients. Summer asked, "What do we do once she no longer needs help? Y'all gone kick us out?" I laughed when Jaxon told me that. I wanted to know what he said when she asked that. "I told her that they could stay there as long as they needed to. The house would be big enough for everyone to have their own space." He explained.

After I thanked him for always putting my needs and loved ones above all his needs and wants, he informed me of Lena's punishment. He said that he sent her back to her country with a black eye she better be glad I only sent her back broke instead of broken in pieces. I asked him who blacked her eye. "Was it you?" I asked. "I don't hit women. The man whom she was working with blacked her eye, and he was whooping her ass when I arrived. Probably because the only safe box she knows about is the one I place grocery money in. Like, how dumb can you be? Every time she opens that safe, it's only holding five hundred for grocery expenses. I put that in there every two and a half months, so there is no way she thought that plan through." Jax explained. I think Lena's plan was to hold me against my will and make me open one of the safes for her. "So, bae, when do you want to move? Talk it over with God, then Elle and Summer. If we move now, I'll need Summer and Elle to come as soon as possible.

No rush, I'm just not leaving you home alone anymore. Even though it'll be a new city and state. Plus, I have some things I'll need to handle before I can stop traveling altogether. I want to go ahead, handle it expeditiously, while the babies are baking. We have a month until the baby shower. Which means I need to get all my shit together." Jaxon said. I guess I dozed off because the conversation ended, and Jaxon nudged me two times. I ignored both. I was too sleepy. The smell of cinnamon, bacon, eggs, maple, and freshly squeezed orange juice fills my room. Eyes still closed, I laid and thought about how much better I would feel if I was to get up and eat. I rolled over and napped for fifteen more minutes before I hear a familiar voice. The person said, "I am going to check on her." I instantly opened my eyes. I'm trying to figure it out without getting up. My room door flew open. "Get up Anna, I made you a variety of things for breakfast. You need to eat before we get on the road. We'll have a pretty long ride." Elle said. I told her good morning and gave her a hug because I couldn't believe she was here. I asked her where we were going, that was so important. "We're moving. Jax left a few pages of homes in the kitchen for you. He said you should pick the one you want, and don't worry about the price. He also left furniture books because he's selling the house fully furnished." Elle replied. I was so happy to see my BFF, but I couldn't help but wonder where could Jax be? I apologized to Elle for being so lazy, so I thought maybe, I should get up and keep her company. It's like I sleep my days away. It feels like I only was sleep for 30 minutes, but in reality I wake up and it's a whole new day. "It's okay . The babies need all the rest they can get. That's why Jax got you an RV for the trip. We'll have a six-and-a-half-hour drive. Get up and eat, then you can sleep comfortably in the RV." Elle said.

She also told me to get my fat ass up, so her godchildren will know more than just eating and sleeping. "Elle is always babying you. Get your booty up." Says Summer. She came in, fussing and rubbing my belly. I asked Elle how come she didn't tell me Summer was here? "Well, Anna, I thought you heard her loud ass come through the door. Summer sold her car, and so did I. So, guess what? I've been with her loud ass since the driver picked us up. Sorry I failed to mention her being here though." Elle said. "I'm loud, and you snore loud. How the fuck are you loud in your sleep? Cow sounding ass bitch. We need to put a muffler on your ass at night." Summer replied. I got up and pushed Summer out of the door. "Oh, yea, breakfast was good, Elle. Wake me when it's time to hit the road. I'll make sure to sleep quietly." Summer boasted. I began going through the cabinets for plates in order to fix my breakfast. These folks weren't playing this morning. I ate my food on plastic even though I hated doing that. It didn't take me long at all. Breakfast was amazing. When finished, I went back to my room to pack a few important items. These bitches have beat me to it. How do they move so fast? I had a pair of shoes out, one outfit, and a phone charger. I went out to the U-Haul and started looking and digging. I looked like a pregnant pirate digging for treasure. I grabbed all my morning essentials. Body wash, toothpaste, washcloth, face wash, bonnet, and of course, my shower speaker. In order to start my day, I need my morning shower. "Like I said, wake me up when it's time to go." Summer said. I yelled at them both and told them to shut up for once. I showered for an hour straight before Elle came in and rudely cut the water off. I turned it back on, and this hoe turned the lights off. I guess I'll have suds in my ass on the road. Jax left me a letter informing me that he would be trailing us. I wasn't worried because he's an honest man who sticks to his word. The crazy part is, as soon as we put the sale sign up, a couple bought our home. Money is never the issue, and neither is trust. A woman never feels bad about following a man who knows how to lead. She never feels played and insecure when she has everything, she needs without having to ask or remind the man who claims to love her. If a man truly loves his wife or girlfriend, he'll put her in a position to be beyond great. He will invest in her in every way physically possible.

A husband is supposed to make you feel like a grand prize. Every day should feel like the first day of the best day of the rest of your life. Marriage should be so joyful that every day feels like your wedding day. When you are happily married, you'll become one and move as one. Nothing can break up this beautiful marriage of mine. No matter what Jax goes through, I'll always be right by his side. The, the same way he is about me. I am ready for whatever challenges that come our way. We'll face them together. I can't wait to start our life in our new home. I was torn between two houses for my top picks. The first was 3 stories, eight bedrooms, eight and a half bathrooms, a pool outside and it had mini indoor pool. It was mainly brick with a tall gate. The second option was ten bedrooms, eleven baths, two pools, family Jacuzzi inside, and a movie theatre. It also had a built -in man cave with a spiral staircase and the ceilings were cathedral. I loved that, and I might just go with that one. Jaxon didn't care, as long as I was happy. I also had plenty of savings, so the price isn't a problem. I took a nap after growing bored from riding.

In the midst of me slobbering, I drifted into a deep sleep and began to dream. Everything seemed normal. I was still pregnant and just woke up for a snack. As soon as my feet touched the cold tile, I walked my lazy ass to the fridge. I grabbed milk and brownies. Afterward, I walk to my bathroom and start to pee. Just when it starts to feel real, I woke up and it was. My pants are soaking wet. What the fuck? I needed him to pull over. "Are you still asleep? This is a freaking RV. Go change and shit in your room or the bathroom." Summer said. I laughed loudly because Summer really did help me come to reality, but the twins were causing me pain. Maybe I needed to lay down. I'd be in the back taking a nap. They knew to text me if they needed me. I changed, but my pain hadn't eased up, not one bit. I laid down and started praying for the twins. I'm whooping their asses' the first chance I get. Lord, forgive me, and please continue to make and mold me. I thanked him for the double blessings and family. Elle and Summer are the only blood/friends I have left. I thanked the Lord for these healthy babies despite the pain. I went to sleep after praying in my bed on the RV.

I woke up on a stretcher leading towards an open emergency door. I thought I was dreaming until I looked to the left of me and saw Summer and Elle both crying. "It's going to be okay. You're in labor." Elle says. "We're right behind you, and Jaxon is on his way." Summer yells as usual. I asked God to help me and to keep my children safe. I even prayed for healthiness upon arrival. "Bless their little lungs and hearts, Lord God. Please, God, be with me." "I prayed. "I made six months today, and I know you're going to protect them regardless of the matter. Despite what the doctors may say, my faith lies with you, Lord. Thank you, Father God, for a safe delivery and healthy children." I continued. I also asked the Lord to be with Jaxon because I know he's doing two-hundred and fifty miles per hour on feet or on a bird's back to get here. He thinks I'm alone, but the twins and I are blessed by the good graces of God. I know he's right here with us. Jaxon will see that in the end, whether he's there to witness their birth or not....

To be continued...

BUT GOD

Before I tell the story on how God counted me in when everyone else counted me out. I just want to Thank God whom happens to be the leader of my life. I want to thank my friends and family who have stood by me through this entire process. My family for encouraging me to follow my dreams and always go for whatever I want in life. My mom often says things that make sense, but also piss me off and push me at the same time. I think most mothers have that effect on their children. It's like the things she say motivate me and make me mad in the same sentence, but I'm very fortunate to have her in my life. Our relationship has changed for the better and I appreciate her for saying whatever the hell she wants no matter how mad I get. I know for a fact she wants the best for me and she has been encouraging me to start writing since I was in middle school. She has always seen my talent for exactly what it was and never pushed the brakes no matter how aggravated I got. I appreciate my friend Nakea for constantly reading over my book and stepping in wherever needed. I appreciate my friend Tracia for donating money towards getting my book published before she could even read it. I appreciate my friend Naquerria for listening to me go on and on about this book and reading chapter after chapter even when she didn't want to. I'm especially thankful for my sisters who push me to become a better version of myself. They believe in me when I'm blinded by foolishness and can't seem to find the strength to believe in myself. They pulled me out of the darkness when I couldn't find the light. They fill me up when I'm running low on self-esteem. They are the reason why my book is being published in this season.

Two years ago I started writing this book. I wrote it out on paper because it's something about watching a pen glide across a blank piece of paper. I like how it feels, I love how I can hold the pages when I'm done, and who doesn't love a good pen that glides at ease? Well at the time I just couldn't put my faith in electronics, because I was too afraid something would get deleted. Crazy part is pages still ended up going missing. This book is like my baby so I sort of was losing my mind over any little thing going wrong . I could sit a to-go cup of soda on the table and would literally get in my feelings if the cup began to leak near the pages. So finding out that I had lost an entire chapter drove me fucking mad. God kept telling me "publish the book." It's like I kept getting daily reminders to make getting my book published my main priority. I would look for publishers, but none of them really were in my price range and all of them seemed to care more about getting the money than they did about catering to my specific needs concerning my child. I felt like I was trying to find the perfect pediatrician or physician to operate on my baby. You don't just leave your child in the hands of a stranger or someone whom you don't trust. You do a thorough background check and you do your research. Well in the midst of me taking my time to research different publishers my home was broke into while I was at work. At the time I was working 12 hour shifts at night. When I came home around 7:15 am I found my apartment door kicked in. The thief mainly took materialistic items because I was running a small boutique from my home so of course it was bound to happen because when you allow people inside your home to shop nine times out of ten one of those people will be studying the place and trying to figure out the best way to steal. I instantly began running around the apartment like a chicken with its head cut off. Not because the majority of my merchandise that I was selling was gone, but because I didn't have a clue of where my book was. I noticed the designer book bag that I normally carried the book in was missing. After a full hour of trying to retrace my steps and collect my thoughts I found my book. I never was really mad about the materialistic items. I was upset about my most prized possession which happened to be my book. That small robbery changed my life forever, and motivated me to start taking my business and writing more seriously. I prayed about the situation and I heard God say in so many words "What he has for me will always be for me and the same way he provided a way for me to buy the materialistic items is the same way he'll provide a way for me to get them back." and last but not least I heard him say look for a publisher on Instagram and get the book published. I spent the majority of my time searching for a publisher on Google so I knew I was hearing from God because as soon as I begin to listen to him I found Dr. Synovia on Instagram. Her packages were affordable and she never took too long to respond to my questions. I just say all of this to say follow God and you'll never go wrong. When you try to do things your own way instead of trusting him to lead your life you'll run into all types of problems and brick walls that will knock you down mentally. It's okay to fall down as long as you get up and learn from your mistakes. It's just like taking a test the more you fail the more you have to retake the test. You can't do the same routine, but expect different results. As people we often get too comfortable and don't realize that being comfortable is what's keeping us behind. Sometimes you have to step outside of your comfort zone and do things you've never done to get the results/ benefits you've always wanted.

Keyonia Dawson

Contact the Author

Keyonia Dawson

Email@ KeyoniaDawson@yahoo.com

Interested in Writing and or Publishing a book?

Contact @Dr.Synovia @www.a2zbookspublishing.net or @Dr.Synovia on Instagram

9 781943 284603